The Will Of

When he pushed the door open to the battle practice room, prince Ahmesh immediately saw several other men on the floor groaning. None seemed seriously hurt, but all were bleeding and battered. Across the room he spied Nefertari. Twirling her stick fluidly, she looked every bit the proud, tall and strong Kemetian princess she was renowned to be. Her long braids wrapped in a tight cloth, Nerfertari wore the traditional stick fighting garb consisting of a cushioned shirt, leather skirt and cloth wrapped knees and elbows. Perspiration glistening from her dark brown skin as she wielded her stick expertly, squaring off against two male fighters who circled her warily. Nefertari taunted one about his lack of manliness, causing him to charge in with an overhead swing as she swiveled, holding her stick close to her torso. When the strike swished past she jabbed the warrior in his exposed rib cage twice, fast as a cobra, with the butt of her stick. As he fell over in pain Nefertari booted him aside, then the other warrior took a step forward to engage her.

"Stop!" cried Ahmesh.

The man hesitated, glanced back and realized who addressed him and stood at attention. Ahmesh was, after all, commander of the Kemetic army and no warrior dared defy him. Nefertari looked over at the prince, rolled her eyes, and then locked gazes with her opponent.

"Keep going atef," she said to the warrior.

"You heard me atef," cried Ahmesh pointing at him, "stop now!"

"And you heard me!" Nefertari growled at the fearful and confused stick fighter. The man looked back and forth at both prince and princess several times, and then he threw down his stick and ran from the room.

For Koff

Princess Nefertari

Peace!
Bu. 9 8/2/22

PRINCESS NEFERTARI
BOOK 1

By Gregory "Brother G" Walker

Published by Seker Nefer Press, a division of Seker Nefer Group

www.africanlegendsinteractive.com

Cover art by Alain Vitus Ndoumbe Nkotto

Graphic Design: Khalidi Lawson

Back cover: Hatshepsut Temple engraving of the great Sheps Nefertari

First Printing 2014

Other Books by Brother G:

Shades of Memnon - Book 1: The African Hero of the Trojan War

Shades of Memnon - Book 2: Ra Force Rising

Shades of Memnon - Book 3: African Atlantis Unbound

Nimrod the Hunter - Book 1

Library of Congress Cataloging-in-Publication data:

Walker, Gregory Lyle

Princess Nefertari

ISBN-13: 978-1500325749 (Original 2014 Softcover Edition)

1, Mythology. 2, Historical Fantasy Fiction. 3, African Studies. 4, Martial Arts. 5, Spirituality

1 Title

PRINCESS NEFERTARI: PROTECTRESS OF THE NILE
BOOK ONE
OF THE NEFERTARI SAGA

AN AFRICAN LEGENDS ADVENTURE

BY

BROTHER G

Brother G (Gregory L. Walker) is the creator of the African Legends genre and a practitioner of the ancient Kemetic Ausarian spiritual system. For the past 24 years, Brother G has done extensive research into ancient Kushite cultures worldwide, with an emphasis on finding heroic icons of the past for literary, educational and multimedia use today. The African Legends genre is designed to restore ignored history and encourage historical self esteem in African youth. A recipient of the 2009 Octavia Butler Humanitarian Award for his ground breaking "Shades of Memnon" series, Brother G is also the author of the critically acclaimed "Nimrod The Hunter" series.

Thanks

Thanks to my beloved Yvonne "Shai" Hankins for her patience and assistance in my writing and publishing endeavors. Thanks to Dr. Akua Gray for the editing assistance and input. Thanks to Ra Un Nefer Amen and the Ausar Auset Society for the teachings and support through the years. And to Queen Mother Maash-t Amm Amen for the inspiration and the Het Heru Healing Dance.

A huge special thanks also to Queen Afua for the great introduction and the many years healing and uplifting our sisters. This work is my humble contribution to help create more Sacred Women.

June 2014

"It was in Africa that the woman rode at the head of her army. It was in Africa that a woman headed a state for the first time. It was in Africa that a woman became a GOD for the first time. And you get hung up with white women's lib that doesn't have a damn thing to do with you at all."
Dr. John Henrik Clarke

Princess Nefertari

Princess Nefertari

TABLE OF CONTENTS

Spiritual perfection can be equated to a time in African history that has been physically present for more than thirty thousand years. It was a time that spanned thirty one dynasties of spiritual growth, mental ascension, emotional stability and the perfection of physical evidence of the above that is still unsurpassed today. Ancient Kemet was a place where seekers were trained to activate the spiritual body to consciously connect with the highest vibration of source. When the mental and emotional capacity of a physical vibration, which is the densest of the creator's manifestations, attains a high enough level, it unites with source energy and creates a view of the world where there are no confines of space, time and limitations. It would be a beautiful thing to live in that way again. But spiritual perfection is more than a notion, it is the result of a knowledge required for purpose living and an unconditional appreciation for instruction is necessary, not to mention a life time of wisdom teachings that span millinium.

The seekers who mastered spiritual perfection of ancient Kemet took to the intense study of academics, medicine, nature survival techniques, physical strength training and myriads of sciences as the basics of growing up strong and ready to take their place in the world when the elders lead them or stepped aside for the youth to meet the challenges of their time. They equipped them with the light of the ninety nine divine powers of the most high by way of one system of living called Maat. Maat as the spiritual guardian of wholeness and balance in the universe is lived within a set of principles that leave no doubt that the victory of life is present. As the nurturer of divine law Maat teaches the spiritual principles of: Truth which is the courage to radiate freely. Reciprocity is giving unconditionally and receiving as there is a need. Harmony is living life in a balanced relationship with all that exists. Order is accepting the stages and plains of existence that all manifestations are given their proper moment in time. Propriety gives the soul the essence to shine as a divine light for all to see. Righteousness is in an acquired force that is used to live as a Divine Energy. And balance created all things equal when each manifestation of the creator's power is living its purpose for creation. So Maat first and all things there after align themselves in perfect submission to the will of the spiritual masters.

To choose a way of life that exemplifies the ways of the Ancients is told in the legends of time. The women and the men whose souls came forth during this golden age had the opportunity to live many life times as ancestors of the ancients, and with each life time the study of the supernatural was an everyday occurrence. Those who accepted the calling of a supernatural possession were trained for either light or dark possession manifestation. Light workers created the balance of power on the Kemetic universe and so the manifestation of Ra illuminated the skies of the Earth. Also a quandary of black power in the vessels of time known as darkness also had its moments to balance the light. However, Earth being a star of light in the midst of the darkness of the grand universe was created to maintain her place and shine through, but as a mother ages even in her grand wisdom and power, she looks to her children to be that channel of immortality that will carry her into eternity so that her light always maintains the balance.

Ancient Kemet's sons and daughters knew their charge and many of them carried the legacy of the most high with great pride. The sons of Kemet by way of the spiritual guardians developed, built and protected. The daughters of Kemet in their feminine divine nurtured, birthed, and protected according to their charge and the girl child had a special place among the culture because of her life giving ability of birth. It was through her womb that the future of the universe was brought forth and she was the keeper of honor for all family life. Therefore, growing up a girl child was magical, because the magic of birth that came through her brought joy everlasting for more than thirty thousand years!

As the feminine reflection of the creator, half of the universe rests in her hands. A girl child can create the balance of both the seen and unseen worlds. Everything she does and says creates a ripple effect of energy, first in her soul, and her soul's vibration builds, stagnates or destroys her family. As a ripple effect her family's vibrations then nurtures, constipates or annihilates the community and the community's vibrations brings wholeness, confusion or fragmentation to the world. She speaks and the universe listens. She loves and the world is blessed. She works and the community expands. She listens and the family is made whole. Magical!

Not only does she provide the magic she is also immersed in her own magical moments; like when she becomes aware there is a thing called status and she holds a place among her people that warrant respect and honor. Or when she realizes that she has the physical and mental ability to achieve everything she applies her will to. She enters womanhood at many stages and rewrites her relationships based on her truth. She willingly, sometimes even as a mystery to herself, goes through profound rites of passages that prepare her to receive the unspoken goddess principles that will enrich her life through the challenges. And the challenges do come like a furious storm that catches the spring time day by surprise. What a girl child does during her time of storm is an awakening to the strength of her power or her profound weaknesses. The choice to prevail or fall deeper into an unprogressive slumber will be the story she will tell those who come after her or the other choice could be the story that she carries to her grave. A girl child who understands her need to balance the light and dark sides of herself brings forth the provocative essence of her divine feminine. To access and use a level of energy undeveloped by the masses is a crowning that few individuals mastered in their lifetime.

This mastery involves seven cycles of The spiritual guardian Ascension with the first being to honor the Wisdom of Meshkenet by accepting the soul's purpose of being born into the physical realm to complete a life cycle as a WOMAN in the world. She ascends with the acceptance of forgetting herself through infancy so that she can relearn the ways of the current world order. The second cycle is Het Heru's Way. As a girl child she receives the love and attention of family in her formative years and she knows quite clearly who she is as the divine feminine, but somehow like Het Heru she loses sight of herself and turns to a way of life that makes the shedding of blood, sweat and tears a minor occurrence compared to the fury that she reeks upon those in her path. The third cycle is Sesheta's Reign. The pages of her history are being written and when she takes the time to review them she may experience an awakening. This stirring light is the memory of the past, the writing on the temple wall that will be eternally remembered. It is also the adding of the finishing touches on her legacy which will either glorify or warn those who read her life line. The forth cycle is Net's Bow, this begins her second phase of life's instructions where she gathers her sisters in good association and wages the internal war against that which stands against Maat. The fifth level of ascension is the Sekhmet Ba, the time has come for healing and she takes opens her legs wide and spreads her arms out to the distance in complete submission to the fires of change. On her sixth journey after making whole herself within herself, she wraps her arms around the world in the Mut Nut Embrace and begins building her relationship with nature. She understands her connection with the animal world and accepts the sacrifices necessary to blend the worlds in harmony. The seventh and final level of ascension is Ast's Bliss. Here she becomes a force of womanhood when she unites with the masculine divine to bring forth the future of the world in her fruits.

The girl child that goes through and grows through into womanhood is the story of women of whose names are recorded in the stones of time and those women whose names were only spoken in a moment of breath as they lived and died. Their stories are the energy on which we live our lives.

The women of ancient Kemet lived by the power of the divine energy and spiritual guardians. The one divine source that manifested into many energies to experience the millions of years of time that has past and that is to come, and though we can't tell the story of all the daughters of the ancient world we can tell of one who has come forth to inspire and amaze us with her magic and times spent in divine ascension. She is one who built a legacy on her words and actions. She is one who was written in the stones of history. She is one who made a place for you to know the way to honor and respect in the world and her name is...Nefertari.

Queen Afua, June 2014

Princess Nefertari - 18th Dynasty

Kemetic Definitions

Atef – Male friend, colleague.

Ausarian -(Oh sah ri an) Spiritual system of ancient Kemet for raising humanity to divinity. See the "Metu Neter" book series by Ra Un Nefer Amen.

Dark Deceased – Troubled spirits in need of spiritual light that haunt the living.

Djahy – (Jaa-hee) ancient city near modern day Palestine.

Geb – the Earth and the neter that personifies the world.

Het – Home

Hittites – A Eurasian people of the Bronze age who were located in what is now modern day Turkey.

Hyksos – (Hick sos) Invaders from east Asia who took over the northern part of the Nile Valley until they were expelled by Kemet's 18th dynasty, founded by Queen Nefertari.

Maat – The neter of divine order and social system of ancient Kemet.

Medjay – Ancient group of Kushites renowned for their nobility, battle skills and tracking abilities located in various places near and along the Nile Valley. They participated in the defeat of the Hyksos, then many moved in to become part of the population of Kemet.

Mut (moot) - Mother, matriarch. The power of motherhood was revered by most Kushite nations, especially ancient Kemet.

Neter – A intelligent force of nature subject to the will of Ausar level men and women. Similar to the concept of angels in the Judaism Christian tradition, they were falsely called "gods" by later cultures.

Sebau (seb ow) – evil, self destructive person.

Sekmet – Protective feminine neter that symbolized motherly protection. At peace called Bast.

Shekem – Great power. Common title of the kings of Kemet, who where required to also be high priests.

Shekem-t - Great female power.

Tehuti (teh hoo ti) – Neter of wisdom.

PRELUDE

When Shekem Sekenen Ra Ahmesh The Mighty finally fell it was from atop a pile of Hyksos bodies.

In the moments leading to his collapse the Asiatic invaders stood in awe as they watched the ebony hued warrior's war cudgel and deadly sickle sword wreak havoc among them, though his body was riddled with arrows. Their elation at the routing of the Theben army turned to fear as rumors about the superhuman nature of some of the Kemetian warriors, particularly the royalty, came to life before them.

As for the mighty Sekenen Ra Ahmesh himself, he sensed it was time. Having reached deeply into his Men Ab, the heart stilling training he had perfected since he was a boy, he had spoken a word of power. That word had infused his entire body with the warrior power of creation, the Herukhuti vibration of the Ra force, just after the first mortal arrow struck him. But now his purpose had been achieved, as a quick glance across the field revealed. His army was now safely across the canal and had set fire to the bridge, having been protected by a rear guard that valiantly chose to sacrifice themselves. Their king was the last alive from that brilliant strategic effort, and though he knew he could endure long enough to kill another dozen Hyksos, he breathed a huge sigh, allowed the Ra enhanced adrenalin to flow away, and finally allowed himself to fall.

But Sekenen Ra Ahmesh tumbled into neither despair nor pain, even as the Asiatics seized him, cruelly snapping off several of the arrow shafts in the process, and dragged him across the field. The ability to remain at peace amidst any situation had long been perfected among the Kemetic people, particularly the royalty. This lived truth, along with the certainty that the body dies and spirit endures, made the Shekem unshakable in meeting his fate. So when Sekenen Ra Ahmesh was finally tossed down in front of the Hyksos king, instead of fear and panic, his mind was so at peace it allowed his current surroundings to fade away in a hazy mist, to be replaced by an overwhelmingly powerful vision:

The dying Shekem found himself witnessing a scene of utter triumph for the Kemetic people and ignominious defeat for the Hyksos. A proud Theben woman, a princess or queen he knew by her clothing and royal bearing, stood flanked by mighty warriors. Cringing before her, on his knees begging, was a wounded Hyksos king. They exchanged words, the princess shoved her finger in his face with a terrible finality, and then the defeated king rose and stumbled across a huge field. There he joined thousands upon thousands of his Asiatic brethren in an apparent exodus. It was clear that they were being banished from Kemet, as what seemed to be the entire population of the Set worshipers, young and old, commoner and royalty, trudged out into the eastern desert. Rows of mighty, ebony skinned warriors flanked the procession, weapons at the ready, poised to skewer any who decided to try to turn back.

But none did. Shoulders stooped, with nothing but the clothes on their backs, the sandals on their feet and a few provisions strapped across their shoulders, the dreaded Hyksos were being driven from a land they had no business invading in the first place. Focusing again on the regal Theban woman, Shekem Sekenen Ra Ahmesh now saw her speaking with a young man who looked very much like her, a prince, who shared her royal bearing and had similar strength of character. Looking closer, Sekenen

Ra Ahmesh noticed she grasped his very own royal war cudgel. Looking even closer, he noted a family resemblance, and realized he was looking at his own kin. Suddenly his peace was augmented by joy at this revelation: That the fruit of his very own loins would one day rise up and prevail! Led by this princess, their land would one day be free of the dreaded foreigners! He only wished the creator would grant him the privilege of knowing her name. But the stinking breath, loud voice and brutal hand of the Hyksos king yanking his head up by the hair pulled him from the vision. Looking up, the Shekem found himself in the war tent of his hateful rival.

"So, Sekenen Ra Ahmesh the mighty has finally fallen," Apepi, king of the Hyksos pronounced as he shook the Shekem's head by his braided locks. "At last the hippo shall be silenced."

"The hippo... will never be silenced," replied the fading Shekem weakly. "One day soon... the hippo will rise up... from the waves of the Nile... and bite your Set worshiping heads off. "

"Large lip from one who will not live to see whether his mouthings will ever come to be," retorted Apepi as he reached out and grasped the cudgel being handed to him, "for you are about to be slain by your own mighty weapon."

"Ha!" replied Shekem Sekenen Ra Ahmesh as he looked up at his own war weapon hovering above his head. "I can only die if my creator dies, so I go for now in peace. Besides, I have already seen the ultimate defeat of your people. "

Apepi, drawing back to strike the fatal blow, hesitated. There was something in the voice of his hated enemy that seemed to be more than just a condemned man's bluster. Apepi detected the conviction of truth in the words of the Shekem.

"Tell me! Speak before you die!" Apepi

growled.

"She will come!" cried Shekem Sekenen Ra Ahmesh the Mighty. "And when she does it will be the end of your reign!"

"Who?" retorted Apepi. "Who will come?"

"I know not her name," the fading Shekem replied, "but she will be... the doom of your vile ruler ship of our northern lands...this I promise you."

"Then we shall deal with her as I deal with you!" cried Apepi as he crushed the cudgel atop the Shekem's skull and watched him convulse and die. "I am not afraid of your stupid prophesies."

But Apepi was lying. He was afraid. As Shekem Sekenen Ra Ahmesh lifted from his now lifeless body, he took a final look at Apepi before leaping into the eternal light. He could see that the king of the Hyksos was fearful and with good reason. For without the bonds of the body holding him back, the Shekem could at last immerse himself in his vision and he knew:

The liberator would be his granddaughter and she would be a woman of immense power - the kind of power not seen since the ancient matrons who helped start the Kemetic people on their path to greatness. Shekem Sekenen Ra Ahmesh could see her clearly now, as his spirit slipped into the land of the ancestors, and he smiled. He could see her and he could finally hear her name as the crowd around her shouted it in joy. The salvation of Kemet and the hope of the world would be known by the name Nefertari!

Chapter 1: What Ever Could They Want With Me?

It was nearly noon and Aten's rays beamed down strongly on the deck of the royal barge as it floated "up south" on the great Red Sea. Next to the large cabin centered on the deck stood a couple of large, burley, brown-skinned men dressed in simple loin cloths. One held a huge peacock feather fan, which he waved vigorously at the small ebony skinned girl lounging atop the velvety reclining couch between the two men. The other servant held up a round, color- ful sun shield on a stick, deflecting the hot rays away from her. Suddenly a large wave dashed against the boat, rocking the vessel and causing the two servants to stumble, momentarily sub- jecting their charge to the unfettered heat of the elements.

The reclining girl's eyes snapped open as she lifted her head, covering her eyes with one small hand. She hissed at her servants, who immediately righted themselves to shield and fan her once again. She shot them both a hard look that said "it better not happen again," be- fore settling back into her nap. Nearby a boy around the same size and age, in fact the little girl's twin, observed his sister with a sour look. He was moving through the warrior exercises he had been trained in by their body guard Tu Ka Na, a wiry, but strong looking little man who stood nearby holding a practice pole. Tu Ka Na's hair was white, but his eyes were still quite sharp. He was observing the little girl too, and considered her the most spoiled child he had known during his service to two generations of Kemetic royalty.

"She will be alright after she goes through her rites," Tu Ka Na said, tossing the pole to his young student.

"I hope so," replied the prince as he caught the pole and began to twirl it. "Because I am not the only one getting tired of her. Our Mut had a terrible time getting her to come along for this, even though she knows it is her royal duty. We must make stronger relations with the Medjay people if we are ever to be free of the Set worshipers. My sister knows this, yet still she continues with her attitude."

Tu Ka Na nodded as he continued to listen, but his attention was now distracted by a small shape floating on the sea that was slowly getting bigger. The shape soon got big enough to let him know it was a ship.

"There!" the elder warrior cried, pointing. "They are coming! Get the princess ready while I go to inform the Queen Mut!"

As Tu Ka Na stepped over to the ship's cabin and gently knocked on the door, the prince walked over to his reclining sister. He waved away the two servants and when the rays of Aten hit the princess again she sat up with a scowl. Peering through her fingers, she spied her brother standing before her.

"What do you want Ahmesh!"

"Time to get ready Nefertari," Ahmesh replied. "The Medjay will be here momentarily."

"Already?"

"Already Nefertari...now get moving..."

"You don't tell me what to do!" Nefertari snapped back. "Remember: I am the oldest..."

"By 10 minutes?" Ahmesh growled, "Sister we are the same age!"

"I emerged first and by tradition you don't tell me what to do..." Nefertari retorted.

"But I do!!" the powerful voice of their Mut boomed out.

Queen Mut Ah Hetep strode toward them, with Tu Ka Na by her side. Dressed for a diplomatic event, she was resplendent in a long, regal white robe draped over a white and gold skirt and blouse. Atop her head sat the gold and black striped royal nemes, centered by the head of the gazing vulture Nekehbet. The queen strode forward with a jackal headed Uas scepter, which, as she looked her children over with disdain, was tamped sharply on the deck to command attention.

TAP!

"I birthed you both so it is I who give orders," the queen continued. "Nefertari, get up and get dressed. You will greet our friends like a proper princess of Kemet. Ahmesh, you were told not to work out before greeting our friends, because you know how you smell afterward. Now get into the cabin, wash yourself off and apply some rosewater.

TAP!

"Now! Both of you- do it quickly or I shall have Tu Ka Na beat you!"

Both children scrambled into the cabin and ran to the private chambers they shared with the Queen. Nefertari began laying clothing out on her bed, while Ahmesh stripped, poured some water into a shallow vase filled with soap powder and began washing himself with a small cloth. There was little space between the bed and wash cabinet, so back to back, the two royal children readied themselves as they had been instructed. While tying some golden thread into her braids, Nefertari glanced over her shoulder, spying her brother's soapy brown naked behind. With a mischievous smirk, she reached around and pinched it, causing Ahmesh to yelp loudly and stand on his toes. The princess continued to fix her hair innocently as Ahmesh grimaced, rubbing his aching butt.

"That's for trying to tell me what to do!" Nefertari giggled.

"I shall be avenged for that treacherous rear attack," Ahmesh replied with a mischievous grin of his own. "You just wait. You'll wake up with sand in your hair, or I'll…"

Just then the queen burst in.

TAP!

"What is going on in here?"

"Nothing Mut!" they both replied innocently.

Moments later the royal family stood silently as the entourage from the boat bobbing next to them began crossing the secured plank linking their vessels. The Medjay honor guard came first- 6 strong, ebony black men draped in red shoulder sashes, wearing purple loincloths and carrying long spears. They took a walk around the entire ship, surveying everything, before settling across from the Kemitic honor guard standing near the royal family. After a nod from the lead warrior, a tall muscular man and young boy crossed over. The man was dressed identically to the other warriors, except for a shining, multicolored collar of royalty covering most of his large barrel chest. The boy wore a purple loincloth and had a bag strapped across his chest via a rope. They stopped in front of the Queen and the children, bowing deeply.

"Hail and greetings Queen Mut Ah Hetep!" both the man and boy said in unison.

"Hail and greetings to you Prince Pakhu," the queen replied. "And who is this little one with you?"

The prince placed his hand on the young boy's back and pushed him forward proudly.

"This is my youngest brother, Prince Keshef," Prince Pakhu replied proudly. "Though his is a mere 12 years breathing, he has passed his rites..."

The queen stepped forward, bending slightly to peer into little Keshef's eyes. She saw what she expected to see: the strength of spirit that the Medjay were famous for. Then she placed a hand upon his little shoulder.

"Salutations, young man!" the queen exhorted, as Nefertari rolled her eyes and Ahmesh shifted uneasily from foot to foot behind her. "I have heard the manhood rites of your people are indeed trying. Did this include the lion trial also?"

Princess Nefertari

The little prince hesitated to answer, and then looked back over his shoulder at his older brother. Prince Pakhu nodded, indicating he had permission to answer a question about their most sacred warrior ritual.

"No Mut," prince Keshef replied. "They just let me bait a lion and rand run away. I am too little yet for the full ritual..."

"Hah!" the queen laughed, "that alone proves your bravery! Let me introduce you to my children, who shall be accompanying your brother back to your home as you come with me to Kemet. This is Princess Nefertari and Prince Ahmesh."

"Hail and greetings prince Ahmesh and princess Nefertari," prince Keshef declared.

The two children stepped forward to bow before the Medjay prince, who was a little shorter than them by two or three fingers stacked. The twins bowed deeply, though Nefertari, instead of looking right at prince Keshef as customary, merely cut her eyes at him and looked away. "Hail and Greetings Prince Keshef," declared Ahmesh.

"Hail Prince Keshef," said Nefertari half-heartedly.

Queen Mut Ah Hetep stamped her scepter upon the deck forcefully.

TAP!

"Nefertari! Proper greeting!"

"Hail and greetings prince Keshef," the princess said correctly.

The queen frowned at Nefertari, giving her the "we will discuss this later" look. Then she turned towards their visitors.

"My apologies friends," the queen stated. "The princess does not relish doing her diplomatic duty to sojourn in your land and learn your ways. She has been impossible..."

Prince Pakhu chuckled.

"Neither did prince Keshef want to come," he

replied. "He can't stand the idea of living in one place all the time. But I did it and he knows he must also. And do not worry about the princess - my Mut and the rest of the Medjay women shall set her right."

"I have no doubt about that," the queen replied with a light laugh. "Now come Prince Pakhu, let us discuss some details."

The Queen Mut and the prince strolled over to the other side of the ship, leaving the children standing together. The children watched them walk away, and then the arguing started.

"Why did you greet him first," Nefertari asked, pointing at her brother and stepping close to the Medjay prince with a frown.

"What?" prince Keshef replied. "I know not what you mean?"

"You greeted him before you greeted me..."

"Nefertari stop..." Ahmesh interjected.

"I greeted you both at the same time," Keshef replied. "with more respect than you greeted me!"

"I did that because you said his name first..."

"What difference does it make?" Ahmesh said.

"I was born first! In our land that means something..." Nefertari cried.

"In our land men are greeted first," retorted Keshef. "unless a higher ranking woman is around."

The Medjay prince turned towards Ahmesh. "Does your sister rank higher than you?"

"No!" Ahmesh cried.

"Yes I do!" countered Nefertari.

"Well you are not acting like it..." replied Keshef. "You don't act like a princess at all..."

"What do you know," retorted Nefertari angrily. "You're just a nafis!"

"Nefertari!" cried Ahmesh, shocked.

"Nafis?" Keshef asked, "what's that?

"You don't want to know..."declared Ahmesh, throwing up his hands. "Sister, you must not say such things about our guest..."

"An insult?" said Keshef angrily, stepping closer to Ahmesh, "Was that an insult? If it was I am going to have to hit you Ahmesh!"

"Me? I didn't say it!" cried Ahmesh.

Keshef took off his bag, set it upon the deck and began flexing his fingers into fists.

"We are not allowed to hit women in my land. But you are her brother so I'll have to hit you..."

"Are you going to let him talk to you like that Ahmesh," Nefertari said with a evil grin. "Throw that nafis off our ship!"

Just then elder Tu Ka Na strolled forward brandishing a practice staff.

"Here now, what is going on?"

"They have insulted a Medjay prince my elder," replied Keshef with a respectful bow. "Such a thing must be answered in battle!"

"I am not afraid of you Medjay tent dweller!" cried Ahmesh puffing out his chest in the presence of his battle instructor. "Name your weapon!"

Nefertari walked over to the elder. Gently taking his hand, she looked up with her eyes innocently widened.

"Elder Tu Ka Na, this foreign boy is acting so terribly! Please tell Mut it is a bad idea to send us to live among such people."

"What kind of fool do you take me for princess," replied the elder with a sly grin. "I know you somehow started all of this. In fact...wait..."

Distracted, the elder peered off into the distance, his eye once again catching something at sea. Then he shouted up at a shipman tying off sails high upon the main mast.

"Shipman! To the west! What do you spy!"

Holding onto the rope he was wrapping around the mast, the shipman peered off into the distance for a moment.

"Two ships, elder," he shouted back down, "coming fast!"

Elder Tu Ka Na let the staff slide from his hand

and clatter to the deck as the children stood trans-fixed. Then he pulled a pouch from his belt. As he leaned down upon one knee, the children forgot about their squabbles and took note of what the elder was doing. Tu Ka Na opened the pouch and shook forth its contents: small slabs of stone about the length of a little finger and wide as a thumb. Each slab had an engraving of a Kemetic neteru, along with other symbols. Tu Ka Na turned all the slabs over to conceal their engravings, and then mixed them together randomly. Closing his eyes for a moment, he picked one slab up, looked at it and frowned. He repeated the entire process over again, then leapt up and ran over to Queen Ah Hetep and Prince Pakhu. All three of them peered off towards the west, then Tu Ka Na began shouting orders at the shipmen.

"What is going on?" asked Keshef.

"The oracles spoke," Ahmesh declared.

"We are in danger," stated Nefertari.

Leaning forward over the bow of one of the approaching ships, Ten Na squinted, causing his burley, brown skinned and bug eyed face to be even more frog-like. As the Kushna War Chief of this expedition, he knew the ships ahead were the prey his war party sought. They were in the right area, doing the right thing just as their informant had said. Now came the time to do what he always hated to do. It was time to go tell the witch.

As he turned away from the ships bobbing in the sea ahead, he barked orders at his men, kicking a couple in their rears that moved too slowly from his path. He thought of sending an underling to inform the Hyksos sorceress that the prize she sought was nearly in their grasp, but half the time he had sent someone before they did not come back. It seemed that Ten Na was the only one aboard that the deadly Hyksos witch considered too important for her bloody sacrificial table. At least that is what Ten Na hoped.

As he got close to the cabin situated mid-deck, the familiar fragrance of incense and death wafted his way, reminding him to do a crew count later. A quick, sharp knock on the door brought forth the eerie voice that chilled the bones of all who heard it:

"Come inside War Chief!"

With one hand upon his long dagger (How did she always know it was him?) Ten Na pushed the door open and stepped inside. As usual his eyes had to adjust to the murky, candle lit darkness of the witch's lair. First he noticed the table due to the flickering lights. It was half covered by a large cloth, half strewn with the strange implements of the witch's dark trade. Then he saw her sitting, as usual, in the high backed chair that looked like it had been carved from ebony wood twisted by giant, angry hands. Her long black gown looked as if it had seeped from the very essence of the chair, wrapping tightly around her surprisingly shapely form. Long sharpened fingernails scraped the arms of her throne, leading up to sleek, copper skinned arms that seemed to disappear into the combined darkness. Her neck and face, floating above the dark dress and chair, was topped off by long, ebony black hair draped over one shoulder. Her face, which was once beautiful, had sallow cheeks and sunken eye sockets, giving the impression of a copper colored skull floating in death-like darkness.

All of this was bad enough, as any one of Ten Na's crew, even the most stalwart and bloodthirsty, could attest, but it was the Hyksos witch's eyes that were the worse. Her eyeballs were black as pitch, surrounded by whites that were as translucent as a long dead corpse's. Ten Na hated being near her, but due to their mutual pact against Kemet, he was forced to report to her and even do her bidding.

"Report!" the raspy voice of the witch commanded.

"Great Set-Priestess," Ten Na replied. "Your

prize is at hand. We are preparing to attack the ships of Kemet and the Medjay now."

"I care nothing for your details. Get me my prize. You do it, personally, not some underling."

Suddenly a long serrated dagger appeared in her hand.

"Fail me and this Set's fang shall taste your flesh."

Ten Na gulped hard. Bowing low, he began backing out of the cabin.

"It shall be done Priestess Nufa Nun," the fearful Kushna leader replied. "We will not fail you."

The ship around the children had suddenly exploded with activity as shipmen ran to and fro shouting. When another ship appeared from the mist, a mood of concern washed like a wave over the shipmen. Doubt about their ability to hold the attackers off took hold, so they turned northeast and began picking up speed toward the land of Djahy. The Medjay ship meanwhile sailed close behind, angling itself to intercept those approaching. As the threatening ships got closer, Queen Mut Ah Hetep and Prince Pakhu finally called the children over.

"Mut, what's happening?" Nefertari asked.

"Someone is coming to attack us," the queen replied. "This meeting was a secret, but somehow word got out."

"But Mut, don't we control all the waters near here?" Ahmesh declared. "Who would dare do such a thing? Didn't we chase away all the pirates?"

"Those are not pirate ships young prince," declared Prince Pakhu. "I recognize those vessels from our dealings with the people of eastern Kush. We knew the Kushna had been forging close ties with the Hyksos. They are most likely coming for your sister."

Nefertari looked up fearfully.

"Me?" she asked, "What ever could they want with me?"

"Nefertari, the Hyksos have been petition-ing for a Theban princess for marriage with one of their princelings for generations," said the Queen Mut. "They know our tradition: that no one can claim true rulership of the Two Lands unless they are legitimized by female Theban blood. Our refusal is one of the main reasons war with them has been unceasing. We must make sure they do not get you child, no matter what."

Everyone looked at Nefertari gravely, as fear crept into her 12 year old heart such as she had never known. Then, the gravity of the situation dawning upon her, she rushed crying into her Mut's arms. How many, Nefertari thought, would likely die to keep her safe?

"I'm sorry Mut, I'm sorry," Nefertari wept.

"There is nothing to be sorry for my child," said Queen Mut Ah Hetep soothingly. "It is those vile Asiatics! They are at fault here..."

Ahmesh stepped forward, placing his hand on Nefertari's shoulder.

"I won't let them get you sister!" he ex-claimed.

"Neither will I little princess," added Prince Pakhu, glancing over towards his younger broth-er. "This attack is an affront to Medjay honor as well."

Prince Keshef stood still for a moment, look-ing from the rapidly approaching ships on the sea to the scared little princess weeping before him. Taking up his shoulder bag, he reached in and pulled out a belt filled with the legendary Medjay throwing darts. The prince draped the belt over his right shoulder, tightened it across his little chest, and then folded his arms in a warrior's stance.

"They will have to come through me to get you princess!" Prince Keshef declared.

Minutes later the sound of battle rang out across the Red Sea as the Queen Mut, Tu Ka Na and the three royal children rowed towards shore in a small boat. The chase was over, the battle begun and Prince Pakhu had stayed behind to help coordinate the fight against the eastern Kushites. In fact, the very last glimpse they caught of the Medjay warrior prince found him laying enemies low with a sickle sword as they rushed across their planks onto the defending ships. Pakhu had given his brother a smile and a nod, and then he was lost in the midst of battle. Prince Keshef had returned the smile and the nod stoically, though he knew it was likely the last time he would see his brother alive.

Taking advantage of the distraction of the battle, Tu Ka Na now rowed his four charges the last mile or so to the shore. The plan was to travel by foot to the Kemetic fort on the outskirts of Djahy for safe haven and report the treachery of the Kushna. But the land was fraught with dangerous bandits on the road and wild animals in the vast forest, making it a·dangerous, long journey for any company of seasoned warriors, let alone a small band such as theirs with children.

"Oh no," cried the Queen Mut, pointing back towards the ships.

As the battle aboard the ships raged, two smaller boats separated from the others and began coming their way. As the first of them rounded the side of their vessel it was riddled with arrows from the Kemetic ship. All the warriors aboard it fell over dead into the water, but the other small boat got by and kept on coming.

"Tu Ka Na!" the Queen Mut said. "Please row faster."

With a grunt, the elder warrior put his back into it, picking up the pace, but the pursuing boat had perhaps six men, and four of them were rowing. Though they were more than halfway to shore, it was clear they would be overtaken before they got there. Tu Ka Na knew this also and racked his mind for a solution. When they got perhaps a ship's length to the shore the old elder shouted:

"Swim children!"

The Queen Mut picked up a bow and a quiver of arrows, handing a sickle sword to Tu Ka Na. As she shot an arrow at the rapidly approaching boatful of enemies, she nodded at Tu Ka Na and addressed the children.

"Yes children, swim to shore while we hold them off. Take whatever food and water you can carry! Do it now!"

"But Mut," Nefertari cried, "what of you and Tu Ka Na?"

"Do as she says! I taught your Mut to fight myself," cried Tu Ka Na. "We will delay them while you get away."

Ahmesh and Nefertari had tears in their eyes as they tied supplies to the backs, while Keshef scanned the shore.

"I will take them to Djahy," the little Medjay prince declared bravely. "To pass my rites I had to survive in the wild alone. I swear to you that I will get them safely to the fort."

Tu Ka Na and the queen looked at each other and nodded their agreement. The elder warrior gave them directions to the fort and handed prince Keshef a bow and a quiver full of tied arrows. Just as Keshef tried to leave, the elder pulled him close, whispering something into his ear. The Medjay boy looked at the elder warrior most gravely, and then nodded and plunged into the water. He was followed by Nefertari and Ahmesh. As they swam away they heard a scream from one of the attackers as the Queen Mut shot him, followed by more shouts, cries and splashes.

When they got to shore they turned around to see Tu Ka Na and the Queen Mut battling hand to hand with two men who had leapt over from their boat. Two other bodies bobbed in the water, but the two other warriors were missing. Nefertari spotted them swimming their way and pointed them out. Keshef notched an arrow, aimed carefully and shot one of them. As the man howled and his companion turned to see to him, the children took a final glance at the Queen Mut and Tu Ka Na fighting. Somehow sensing they were looking instead of running, the Queen Mut screamed out loudly as she fought:

"Go! Get away from here children! Go now!"

The children took off across the sand, headed for the forest and ran into the trees with the sound of battle following them.

Chapter 2: A More Dangerous Pack

Ten Na was astounded at the accuracy of the arrow shot at them by the little Medjay boy. It actually whizzed past close enough for him to feel it near his ear. It missed him though, plunging into the shoulder of the warrior swimming next to him in their pursuit of the children. Not knowing if the wretched child would follow the shot with another, Ten Na swam back to the wounded man under the pretext of concern, while actually using his body as a shield. When the man started to convulse Ten Na simply held his face under water until he stopped, continuing to hide behind his still frame as the children took off for the forest.

With a brief glance behind him Ten Na noticed the pitched battle between the boats and the closer fight between his warriors and a Kemite woman and old man. Shrugging his shoulders, the Kushna chief decided that his men could handle the situation and pressed on. Pushing past the limp body of his human shield, Ten Na knew that catching the little princess was his only course of action. Her little royal companions could be ransomed and he would avoid the wrath of that horrible Hyksos witch by bringing her back. But as he splashed from the water onto shore the Kushna chief touched his ear, considering the accuracy of the arrow that had nearly slain him. He then pondered that he just might have to kill the Medjay boy despite the promise of ransom.

Meanwhile the children made for the forest and kept running for a long time. Several times Nefertari stopped to sob against a tree, but Ahmesh would quickly console her and they would run on. After the seventh tearful delay though, Keshef had had enough. Grinding his fleet little feet to a halt just past the tree they leaned against, he turned on the twins with a serious look of disdain.

"Ahmesh get your sister going," the little Medjay prince cried. "We don't have time for this..."

"Give us a moment!" Ahmesh returned as he held his sobbing sister.

"We don't have a moment!" roared Keshef. "That other Kushna is coming for us, of that you can be sure!"

"We may have just lost our Mut Medjay!"

"And I most likely have lost my brother!"

"You're heartless!" Nefertari cried, looking up from her brother's tear soaked shoulder.

"My heart is still!" replied Keshef. "My brother taught me Men Ab after he learned it in Kemet! You are Kemetic royalty! You should be stilling those feelings with proper breathing too..."

Ahmesh stood up with his hands on his hips.

"I am doing it Medjay, but Nefertari has not gone through her rites, so she is not very good at it yet."

"Well consider this her rite of passage then. After we lose this Kushna we can settle down and practice together," growled Keshef, stepping towards them. "But now you had better get her up, or I shall drag her by her braids to her feet!"

Ahmesh took a step towards Keshef menacingly.

"You'll not touch my sister tent dweller!"

"Elder Tu Ka Na put me in charge and I will do whatever I must to get you two to Djahy!"

"Why are you so mean Keshef?" Nefertari sniffled.

"Mean? Don't you know what is at stake here?" Keshef shot back. "We can't let them get you and force you to marry a Hyksos prince!"

"My sister would never do such a thing!" hissed Ahmesh.

"Never would I marry one of them!" Nefertari added.

Keshef rolled his eyes.

"You two have really led sheltered lives

haven't you? They have ways...torture... or they will cloud your mind somehow..."

"Not my mind," cried Nefertari. "I would die first..."

Keshef stepped closer, pointing directly into Nefertari's face.

"Well I am glad you feel that way, because they told me to make sure you are not taken alive!"

Keshef was immediately sorry he said this, as suddenly a shocked silence came over the children. The twins looked at each other for a long moment. Then Ahmesh spoke up.

"That is what elder Tu Ka Na whispered to you?"

"It was," replied Keshef grimly. "It was a directive straight from you Mut. We cannot let them take her to the Hyksos."

Ahmesh was about to speak again, but Nefertari shook his shoulder, silencing him.

"They were right," she declared. "I am a princess of Kemet. I cannot allow myself to be used for the downfall of my people."

Suddenly a loud gruff voice rang out from somewhere nearby.

"Well it is too late for that!"

Ten Na stepped from behind a tree, flexing a bow, an arrow notched and pointed at the children.

"Do be a good girl princess and step over to me, or I will shoot your brother in the heart."

"I told you!" declared Keshef. "While we were running our mouths this sneaky Kushna cur caught up with us..."

"Shut up boy or I will forgo ransom and shoot you now," Ten Na growled. "Princess, get over here or your brother dies..."

Suddenly Keshef pounced upon Ahmesh, knocking him to the ground. Ten Na let fly but the arrow flew harmlessly over them.

"Run Nefertari!" Both boys shouted.

Nefertari bounded away and the Kushna

took off after her. Keshef jumped to his feet, extending a hand to pull Ahmesh up, and they charged right after him.

Nefertari was fast. Her little feet a blur, she dodged roots, leapt over small bushes and ducked branches to gain a good lead over the enemy warrior chasing her. But she could sense his relentlessness and knew it was only a matter of time before she tripped or got tired and he would have her. She knew also that her brother and the Medjay boy would be close behind and that together they might have a chance against him. So as she ran, the princess looked for any advantage she could to slow him down.

After dodging a large bush filled with dangerous looking thorns she thought she had the answer. Turning back to the thorny bush, she carefully tugged at a couple of its branches. Listening intently to gauge how close her pursuer was, she decided she had time to set her trap. Seizing a couple of long, thick branches filled with fang-like spikes, she slowly and carefully pulled them. Bending them back like a bow string, she tilted the branches down towards another leafy bush which she hid behind.

Nefertari only had to wait a few seconds before the large ugly man came charging, unwittingly lining himself up for her surprise. Just as he appeared she yanked the branch back with a final hearty tug and let go.

Ten Na was irritated. He'd had just about enough of all the running. He was so angry that he decided that one of the boys would have to die despite the promise of royal ransom. Up ahead he heard the girl stop, most likely a futile attempt to try and hide. This made the Kushna grin, for his people were renowned trackers almost on the level of the Medjay, and it would not take long to find her. He would have her and then he would coax the two boys close and take out his ire upon one of them. But as he ran past a particularly large bush, two branches sprang forth like bolts of lightning, smashing directly into his face. The impact was tremendous and long sharp thorns sunk into his upper chest, skewering his right cheek to the bone and stabbing into one of his frog-like eyes. The pain was excruciating! And, oh how Ten Na howled!

As Ten Na sunk groaning to the ground he painfully pried at the thorns in his flesh and useless eye. After writhing for a moment he looked up, his good orb widening as the three children gathered around him. The girl wore a shocked expression; apparently surprised at the amount of carnage her trap had caused. The two boys looked down, speaking to each other with absolute delight. Finally, after nodding in agreement, each lifted a foot above the screaming man's head. Their descending sandal heels were the last thing Ten Na saw before darkness overtook him and his screaming stopped.

When Ten Na came back to his senses sometime later he was surprised to be alive. He found himself sitting up, tied to a tree. He was bound hand and foot, and a bandage was over his lost eye. Night had fallen, they were in a clearing and a few yards away the three children sat before a large fire.

The Medjay boy was petitioning for his demise.

"Look, I say again," Keshef argued, "we should tie some stones to his feet and sink him to the bottom of that lake we passed..."

"And I say," replied Ahmesh, "that we should take him to the Djahy fort."

"As much as I hate to admit it," Nefertari added, "I agree with my brother. The man may have useful information about plots against both our people."

Keshef snatched one of the Medjay darts from the band around his chest and began tossing it from one hand to the other.

"Well, just let me get the information from him - and then we toss him in the river! That way we won't have to share our food with him on the way. Did either of you think about that? Well did you?"

"It is not the Ausarian way to just kill people Keshef," said Nefertari.

"Well it is the Kushna way!" pressed Keshef. "And we are not in Kemet! We are in a forest filled with wild dangerous animals and one of them is this Kushna who just tried to kill us!"

Keshef twirled the throwing dart high, deftly catching it between his finger and thumb.

"Let me just poke him in the throat and have done with it..."

Suddenly there came the sound of a throat being cleared and the children looked over to their tied prisoner.

"I have an idea," Ten Na interjected. "I've already lost an eye... and I am pretty badly injured. Why not just let me go and we can all go our separate ways in peace? You Ausarians believe in peace right?"

The children all looked at each other, frowning and grimacing. Then Nefertari got up and took the throwing dart from Keshef's hand. She walked over to Ten Na, whose good eye widened as he gulped fearfully. The princess then sliced off strips of his clothing, stuffing a wad of it between his teeth. Tying a strip around the lower part of the warrior's face, she yanked it tight and walked back to the others. After working out watch details, they took turns sleeping around the fire for the rest of the night - in peace.

Aten arose, the camp stirred and the Kushna warrior woke up, his tightly tied limbs stiff and aching. Much to his relief, Ten Na found the Medjay boy had forgone slicing his throat, which was precisely what he'd have done had destiny's spear been pointed in the other direction. For this he was grateful, but much to his chagrin, he found himself the party's dedicated pack animal. As they set off on the day's journey, his hands were bound behind him and all food and gear was strapped to his burley back. Completing his humiliation, the princess whom he had been sent to capture yanked him along by a rope tied around the neck. Off they went through the dense forest, as branches smacked the Kushna repeatedly about his helpless, injured face.

"Please untie my hands," Ten Na cried at one point, "What if I get unbalanced or trip on a root?"

"Then use your ugly face to break your fall Kushna," Ahmesh declared, causing laughter all around.

After a morning long debate the Medjay boy finally ceased his petitions to do Ten Na in. But only after it was agreed upon that, in the event of an animal attack, the Kushna would be left as bait while the rest of them ran for it. The issue of wild beasts was a frequent subject of conversation as their trek went on, and with good reason. By the third day Keshef noticed they were being stalked.

"Something is following us," the Medjay boy declared as they were making their way through an especially thick part of the forest.

"How do you know?" asked Nefertari, looking around warily.

"Yes, how can you tell?" added Ahmesh.

"The silence," declared Ten Na.

Keshef looked at the Kushna with a grimace, nodding at their prisoner with new found respect.

"As he said," Keshef replied, tilting his chin at Ten Na. "When great prey is stalked by a great beast, the forest becomes still, each creature paralyzed by the fear that it could be next. There has been silence around us for too long. Something is following us."

Nefertari and Ahmesh looked around fearfully.

"What are we to do?" the princess asked.

"We must find high ground, or some place with our backs to water or a wall, before nightfall," Keshef declared. "Then we try to find out what the beast is..."

"There," Ten Na declared, looking toward the northeast. "I saw water birds in the sky descending that way."

Nefertari and Ahmesh looked at Keshef and he nodded his confirmation.

"Then let us go that way. You are being very helpful Kushna," Nefertari declared suspiciously as she tugged on her captive's rope.

"That is because I know I'd be the first tidbit tossed out," Ten Na answered with a grim smile.

As they made their way it soon became apparent, even to the twins, that something was following them. It was a strange, palpable feeling, like something breathing near your neck that disappears upon turning around. As they came closer to the water, ducks and other birds took off. Soon they were standing on the bank of a good sized river, right on an outward bend where it narrowed.

"Why don't we just swim across here where it is smaller?" asked Nefertari. "Perhaps whatever is hunting us doesn't like water."

"And what if it loves water and crosses over after us?" Keshef asked in return. "No, we make our stand here. Gather as much wood as you can. We need to make five large fires..."

The twins hurriedly dragged wood from the edge of the forest to the shore, as Keshef walked back and forth holding a bow with a notched arrow, looking intensely back the way they had come. After a while Ahmesh took his place with the bow, as the Medjay prince knelt to make fire with a hearth stick and dried dung from his bag. As the day grew dimmer and Aten drew nearer to the horizon, they all saw flashes of stealthy movement in the trees. Ten Na looked on with a dire expression for a while. Then he finally decided to speak up.

"Wolves!" the Kushna blared mournfully. "By the gods we are indeed all doomed!"

"Don't listen to that fool," Keshef said, taking up a flaming stick. "Nefertari, arrange the wood into five piles, in a half circle around us. Ahmesh light them with this..."

"A fire fence?" blurted Ten Na. "There is an entire pack out there! You expect to hold them all off with a fire fence?"

"Yes I do!"

"But even if we do have enough wood to last through the night, by morning the flames will burn out and they will be upon us!"

Keshef ignored the Kushna and joined the twins in setting fire to the five large piles of wood in a half circle around them. As they got the flames roaring the final light of day faded and the darkness deepened. Then they could see more than a dozen pair of eyes peering in hungrily from the forest. Suddenly there was a series of eerie, blood chilling howls.

"Owwwwwwwwwwooooooooooo! Owwwwwwwww-wooooooooooo! Owwwwwwwwwwooooooooooo!"

The children stood stock still inside the half circle of fire, the flaming light flickering against their little brown bodies. Ahmesh held a sickle sword, Nefertari held a large dagger and in the middle stood Keshef wielding a bow. His notched arrow was pointing at one of the shadowy, four legged figures slowly emerging from the forest. Ten Na stood behind them, nearly petrified with fear. Shaking in his sandals, he cried out

"Loose me and give me a weapon!"

"Shut up Kushna!" cried Keshef. "I'd feed you to them now if it would do any good. But they would just eat you and keep on coming."

Grinding his teeth defiantly, the Medjay boy looked at his two companions gravely.

"That howl was meant to unnerve us, to get us to run, but they won't come near those fires! We must hold our ground!"

A shadowy canine figure, much larger than

all the others, could be seen toward the rear of the pack. After a growling snap from this figure, three of the wolves edged towards the light. The illumination revealed them as large reddish gray animals, with big triangular ears, cold, piercing gray eyes and mouths full of dagger like fangs.

"What are you waiting for," cried Ten Na fearfully, "shoot!

Keshef simply ignored the Kushna.

"Hold steady everyone," he said quietly.

Several more wolves crept closer to the light. Still Keshef held his shot.

"Medjay, what are you doing?" asked Ahmesh.

"It looks like they are massing for a rush Keshef!" Nefertari said. "You've got to start shooting them!"

Keshef held still, grinding his teeth in concentration. Perspiration slicked his brow from the strain of keeping the bow drawn.

"Not yet Nefertari," he answered in a low voice. "When dealing with a pack, the trick is to shoot the right one first..."

Now almost all of the wolves had come into the light, except the apparent leader. This shadowed wolf goaded the others even closer by growling and snapping at their heels.

""Shoot Medjay!" cried Ten Na. "They are about to overrun us!"

"They are not going to come near those flames Kushna!" Keshef growled back. "They are trying to make us run! Just shut up and let me concentrate!"

Suddenly the pack leader emerged into the light. Grey eyes shining with a hungry malevolence, the big wolf's nose snapped upward to emit another howl, causing the entire pack to immediately join in.

"Owwwwwwwwwwwoooooooooooo!"

It was his last howl, because then Keshef let fly.

The arrow plunged into the exposed throat of the pack leader, transforming its hunting howl into a strangled yelp of pain. Then the big wolf fell dead, causing the rest of the pack to cease howling as they turned in mass to survey their leader. Sad yelps and whines replaced aggressive hunting noises as one after another they sniffed the body.

"Now," shouted Keshef, "If you want to live out the night my friends, take up a flaming log and follow me. Blind them with the fire! Make lots of noise! Kill every wolf I wound!"

Nefertari and Ahmesh both snatched up burning pieces of wood and tightened their grips on their weapons

"Still your hearts my friends! Let us show these beasts what it means to threaten warriors of Kemet and Medjay! Now!"

Keshef let fly with arrow after arrow, wounding many of the wolves as they sniffed at their dead pack leader, while the twins ran forward, screaming and waving fire. Confused and leaderless, the unwounded canines yipped and whined in fear as the hated flames leapt towards them, accompanied by screaming war cries from creatures they thought would be easy prey. Those that could scattered into the forest, further spurned on by the painful howls of their wounded pack mates.

The royal twins fell upon the unlucky wounded wolves with a vengeance –clubbing, kicking, burning and stabbing to save their lives. They fell into the required tactic almost instinctively: One twin would shove a burning torch towards grey feral eyes, thus distracting a fang filled muzzle as the other twin hacked away. When his arrows ran out Keshef joined the melee, smashing canine heads with the bow and riddling them with deadly Medjay throwing darts. The fighting was brutal and intense, but after a few moments it was over and 8 wolves lay dead all around them. Huffing and puffing, the children stood back to back holding their flaming torches aloft, peering into the darkness of the forest.

Ten Na, never having moved from the protection of the fire fence, stood looking on in gape mouthed astonishment.

The children stood very still, waiting until the sounds of the forest returned. After the forest came back to life they waited even a little longer. When it was clear the wolves were not coming back, Keshef walked over to the body of the pack leader. Placing his foot atop the creatures head, he raised his bow and let out a howl that nearly duplicated the cry of the wolves.

"Owwwwwwwwwwooooooooooo!"

The twins looked at the Medjay boy with shock and amazement.

"Come," Keshef beckoned, "this will let other creatures know that there is a more dangerous pack roaming these forests: Us!

The twins nodded and joined him, placing their feet too atop the dead animal's head and raising their weapons also. Then they too threw their heads back.

"Owwwwwwwwwwooooooooooo!" the children howled, "Owwwwwwwwwwwwooooooooooo! Owwwwwwwwwwwoooooooooooo, Owwwwwwwww-wooooooooooo, Owwwwwwwwwwwoooooooooooo!!!"

For the next few days the battle with the wolves was all Ten Na could talk about. Over hills and through valleys, wading rivers and huddled near fires for the night, their Kushna captive went on and on about the impossible way the children had fought off the wolves. As they sat before a night fire six days after the battle, the Kushna still would not stop talking about it.

"The world needs to know of this!" Ten Na cried. "If I had not seen it with my own eyes, I mean eye, I would not have believed it myself. Let me go and I will tell the story to everyone! They will believe me because we are enemies. Just let me go and I will spread your fame everywhere!"

Nefertari rolled her eyes and took out the gagging cloths. As she approached Ten Na he shook his head.

"No," he cried. "Please hear me out. What is one poor wretch like me given to the fort at Djahy compared to the fame you would have if you let me go?"

"Nice try Kushna," Nefertari said, preparing to tie the cloth around his mouth. "But we are all royalty. We're already famous."

"But such valor leads to heroic fame, and heroic fame leads to fortune," Ten Na cried, turning toward Keshef. "What about you Medjay? Don't you want to live in a palace instead of a ratty tent?"

Keshef leapt to his feet, but was held back by Ahmesh

"Tie his mouth tight princess," the Medjay boy said through grinding jaws, "before I kick his teeth in."

Nefertari gagged Ten Na and settled back down near the fire. She looked back and forth at her brother and the Medjay boy for long moments. Then she finally spoke up.

"We are running out of food," she said, thumbing over her shoulder towards the captive, "rapidly because we are sharing it with him."

"I told you," grumbled Keshef. "We should have tossed him in that lake..."

"We will simply get more food," Nefertari declared. "And to help I would like to learn how to hunt and to defend myself like Medjay."

"Then I shall teach you!" declared Keshef vigorously.

"Wait a moment," interjected Ahmesh. "I know how to hunt and you don't need to fight because I'm here Nefertari..."

"But what if you were not here brother," Nefertari replied. "What then?"

Ahmesh bristled.

"You know we don't normally teach women

battle skills in Kemet. But if you must, then I shall teach you these things myself!"

"I know Tu Ka Na has taught you well Ahmesh," Nefertari went on, but we are in the wilderness and the Medjay thrive in such places. I would learn the ways of the Medjay."

Keshef carefully observed the exchange between the twins. Then he spoke up.

"Look, we will both teach her!"

"What?" replied Ahmesh.

"We are still weeks away from Djahy with low supplies," the Medjay boy replied. "There are still animals to contend with and maybe even bandits if we get near a road. I too have been thinking that we need to sharpen our own skills and show your sister how to really defend herself."

Ahmesh put his hand to his chin.

"It makes sense..."

Keshef raised a finger, pointing it back and forth between himself and Ahmesh.

"I learn from you and you learn from me..."

"And I learn from both of you!" Nefertari concluded. "Let us begin in the morning."

The next morning the children started with the Aten drills, battle exercises designed to combine the power of the new day with the life force. Known by both Medjay and Kemetic warriors, this activity consisted of graceful body movements designed to strengthen the heart, lungs and other organs by drawing in the power of the newly risen orb of Aten. As the days went on this was followed by stick fighting drills, fist fighting and wrestling. After getting used to the bumps and bruises, Nefertari found that she was especially good at wrestling, with a natural knack for the shifting of weights and quick, tricky movement.

Keshef taught the twins the rudimentary skills of the famed Medjay foot fighting also. Although to be proficient, he informed Nefertari and Ahmesh, would take years, he taught them the basic poses and strikes. Keshef also introduced them to some of the sneaky Medjay weaponry, including the wrist blades, toe blades and heel blades chipped from flint rock. Though the twins doubted the small knives at first glance, they could not deny their efficiency after seeing Keshef slice down bushes and flay the bark off trees with astonishing precision. These sly war implements, painted like decorations adorning arms and notched into sandals, were truly deadly when used by a skilled Medjay foot fighter, and even for those less skilled like the twins, the hidden blades could still prove quite formidable.

The boys taught Nefertari archery also as they trekked through the forest, pointing out targets on the run to train her eyes and reflexes. After fifteen days she shot her first duck, which they roasted over a fire that night. Five days later the princess shot a panther trying to steal another bird she had just brought down. She had aimed for the cat's vitals, but got it in its hind parts, which elicited howls of laughter from the others as it ran away. Still she chased the animal off and they all congratulated her for it. Nefertari's stubborn, tenacious ways that had gotten her into so much trouble growing up in Kemet, proved priceless as she learned the skills of survival in the wild.

Meanwhile, in a dark, hidden place somewhere in lower Kemet, an enraged Nufa Nun paced back and forth in a candle lit chamber. The Hyksos priestess thought back on how she had seized and sacrificed the shipman that reported to her that the Kushna vessel she journeyed upon had to retreat. The doomed man informed her that the Medjay and Kemetic ships had put up a much better fight than they had expected, and that a patrolling warship from Kemet was spotted on the way. As they withdrew she had slain the man, sacrificing him to Set in a fit of rage, all the while wishing he had been that idiotic War Chief Ten Na. The Set priestess had immediately hated the Kushna War Chief, and planned to sacrifice him the minute he got back with the princess. But he did not come back at all, and for that she hated him even more.

Since then several more men had fallen under Set's fang. Half of them legitimate and timely blood sacrifices to the god of chaos, the other half to assuage her rage over Ten Na's failure, which forced her into returning to Avaris without the princess. As one of the Dread Three, Set's chosen triumvirate, she had no fear of the normal fate meted out for failure, but she had sworn to her Dread sisters that she would find a way to get princess Nefertari. The fate of the Hyksos, she knew, depended upon it.

Walking past her latest victim to be, an ebony skinned Kemetic warrior drugged to stupor on Set's alter, the priestess stalked into her dank library. There she consulted ancient, dusty papyri - Hyksos tomes from before the great settling, for hours until she finally thought she had the answer: she would call upon one of the Darkest Deceased, indeed one of the great teachers who first taught the Hyksos the ways of Set. Enlisting the help of this spirit, the Dread sister reasoned, should finally push events towards the way of the great prophesies. Priestess Nufa Nun smiled, because the ritual to summon the dark spirit required only Set-knowledge and blood. As a priestess of Set she was a fount of such knowledge, and blood she had also. Blood she had aplenty.

Princess Nefertari

Chapter 3: We Are Sisters Nefertari!

After weeks of travel the forest at last began to thin, giving rise to a system of lightly forested hills. This was the landmark, Keshef had been told, indicating that they were only days away from the fort at Djahy. But it also meant increased danger from possible bandits stalking the nearby roads. So it was decided to approach the hills near dusk and shelter in one of the many caves described by elder Tu Ka Na. The children found a suitable cave in short order, checked it for animals and settled in for the night. As they huddled near its mouth next to a small fire, all noted an especially sad look on the face of their prisoner. Tightly bound hand and foot as he was nightly, Ten Na glared sourly at the flickering flames.

"I don't blame you for being sad Kushna," Keshef scolded as he shook a finger, "but being delivered to the fort is your own doing."

"I wish I had never set eyes on you three," Ten Na grumbled. "I wish I had never taken this assignment..."

"Why did you take this asignment?" asked Nefertari sitting up, "Don't you know how terrible the Hyksos are?"

"The Hyksos have vast riches," declared Ten Na, "and they pay well to get what they want."

"And when they don't get what they want," Ahmesh said with a wicked grin, "you get this."

Ahmesh got down on his knees, assuming a condemned man's pose. Then he pulled his hand across his throat in a cutting gesture, lolling his head to the side. Everyone nodded in agreement, including the Kushna.

"That is so, that is so," he replied thoughtfully. "but life is risk. No one gets rich without some sacrifice."

Nefertari shook her head.

"The Hyksos don't believe anything happens without sacrifice: the sacrifice of people on alters of Set. They have taken a neter we know as the representation of disorder and made it their neter of all the things. Those vile Asiatics are a plague upon the earth, yet you, our Kushna cousins from our ancient Kushau ancestors, ally with them."

"As I said their gold is good," shot back Ten Na.

"But the Hyksos worship disorder - the opposite of Maat!" Nefertari pressed. "How can that be good for anyone?"

Keshef stood up. Stretching his arms, he let forth a big yawn.

"Just gag this foolish man so that we can have some peace," he declared, "He is a Sebau, a fallen man from a fallen people. You are not going to change him with a lecture. The Medjay have a saying: "A Sebau gains his wisdom through the lessons of the blade."

Nefertari and Ahmesh nodded in agreement, gagged Ten Na, set a watch detail and settled in to rest. Ahmesh was first up, and as he walked the perimeter Ten Na stared at the Medjay child sleeping across the camp, bitter hatred streaming from his one eye. He was Sebau and he knew it. He had always known it. But no one had ever been bold enough to tell him to his face. Ten Na had disliked the Medjay boy before, but now truly hated him. As the Kushna drifted off to a fitful sleep, he vowed to find a way to kill the boy and fulfill his mission, or die trying.

The next day they finally spotted the road, but stayed well away inside the increasingly scant cover of the scrub brush covered hills. All roads near Djahy were renowned for danger, and the children dared not walk it until the last possible hours of travel. So they traversed the increasingly rugged hills through an area that became drier as they went along, while their food supplies got dangerously low. On the fifth day in the hill country the boys left a protesting Nefertari with the prisoner to hunt the hares

Princess Nefertari

they had seen dashing about the hills. It was late day when they tromped off, the best time to hunt the scampering creatures and near the end of an especially long day for Nefertari. Ten Na had been donkey-like stubborn all day, causing her to drag him along, tiring the princess out. With no food left, the princess was both exhausted and hungry, so she yanked his rope downward and both of them plopped to the ground.

"Why are you being so defiant Ten Na?" Nefertari asked. "Your fate is sealed. Just accept it."

"I don't relish being given over to my enemies..." the Kushna grumbled. "And besides, I'm hungry..."

"No one else has had anything to eat today, so stop complaining," the princess grumped back in return.

Ten Na sighed, and then tilted his head back the way they had come.

"I saw a bush back there. It had berries..."

"Keshef said not to trust any plants near these hills to eat," the princess retorted.

"But there were birds eating off it..." the Kushna retorted back.

"Birds?" Nefertari asked skeptically. "Are you sure?"

"Yes I am sure."

"Well why did you not say something earlier?"

"Because the Medjay boy would not have gone along..."

"What makes you think I will?" returned Nefertari.

Ten Na shook his head, looking hungry and pitiful.

"The Medjay boy is proud. So proud he has us starving. What if they don't come back with any game?"

Nefertari thought for a minute, contemplating her own grumbling belly. She did not like being left out of the hunt and disliked not contributing even more. So she tugged at Ten Na's rope and they set off to find the bush.

After nearly half an hour Ten Na led her to the side of a small hill and there it was. Small birds indeed took off from it as they got near. It was a waist high, sturdy looking bush with small purple blooms and delicious looking red berries. Nefertari reached out to take one, then stepped back and looked at Ten Na suspiciously. The Kushna, grinning sheepishly, bowed to her and nodded at the bush.

"After you princess…"

Nefertari plucked a handful of the succulent looking berries, which also smelled wonderful, and drew them towards her mouth. But at the last second she pulled out her dagger and shoved the berries towards Ten Na's face. Lowering her weapon, she dipped the tip of the blade under his waist cloth, holding the cold metal against his groin.

"Now, eat them!" Nefertari demanded.

Sweat poured down Ten Na's neck as he realized his plan had turned upon him. The Kushna knew full well that these particular berries were not safe to eat. In fact, experienced travelers called the bush "the fool's feast" because the fruits were known to cause mental derangement and often even death. Ten Na had spotted the bush earlier, and with his delivery to the fort looming, had decided on this last desperate move. But now he found himself caught between eating "fool's feast" himself and the sharp dagger now pricking his manhood.

With no other choice, the Kushna decided to eat the berries, praying his stronger constitution would overcome the effects and lead the princess to think they were safe. They would both get sick, of that he had no doubt, but if his gamble paid off he'd recover first, use Nefertari's blade to cut free and carry her away. Then he'd spring a trap on the others, kill that wretched Medjay boy and ransom the prince. He could accomplish his purpose, earn a tidy profit and get satisfying revenge. But none of it would be possible if he did not get the princess to eat the berries.

So Ten Na chomped the fruit down with relish as Nefertari drew the sharp bronze away from his privates. The princess observed him carefully as he swallowed, then looked back down with a hungry grin.

"Can I please have some more?" he asked.

"You'll not hog them all Kushna!" Nefertari declared, sheathing her dagger and plucking berries for her own rumbling belly.

The princess downed a handful and started to reach for more when suddenly she heard a mournful groan. Looking back at Ten Na, she noticed his legs tottering beneath him. He took a step towards her menacingly, and then toppled to the ground face first. Suddenly Nefertari's legs began to quiver also, and her head began to swim. She tried to call out to her brother and to Keshef, but her tongue felt swollen. Looking down at the quivering Kushna, she realized she had been fooled and tried to kick him. Lifting her foot only made her lose balance and she tumbled atop him. The foul, musty body odor of Ten Na was the last thing Nefertari noticed before unconsciousness overtook her.

"Nefertari!" Ahmesh cried. "Nefertari where are you!"

"Stop shouting like a fool!" ordered Keshef. "You'll attract every bandit in the region."

Dusk had fallen, and the boys walked back and forth near the place they had left Nefertari and Ten Na. Both had a long legged, floppy eared dead hare strapped across his back, along with the bow that felled it. As Aten crept below the horizon the shadows grew long - too long, both boys realized, for the beginning of a serious search.

Ahmesh shook his head in confusion.

"Perhaps Nefertari found a better place to camp, thinking we would get back in time to follow her."

"She was alone with that Kushna and I'd wager he is somehow behind this," replied Keshef with concern. "Because the princess knows better..."

"What if bandits got after them?" Ahmesh threw out.

Keshef rubbed his little hairless chin.

"I do not think so. Before the light faded I saw no other footprints. Regardless it is turning nightfall now and stumbling about in the dark will do no one any good. Let us dress this game and cook it."

The boys made a small fire, then dressed, cooked and ate one of the hares. They talked for a long while, with Keshef bringing up a surprising subject at one point.

"You know, as a prince of the Medjay, I could get your family perhaps 2 or 3 thousand cattle..."

Ahmesh sat back in astonishment.

"You are not saying what I think you are saying..."

"Sure I am. Your sister would make a good wife," Keshef replied. "Perhaps even a great First Wife."

"Has there been something going on during the times I was out hunting?" Ahmesh asked, pointing and narrowing his eyes suspiciously.

Keshef chuckled, holding up his hands defensively.

"No, my friend, nothing of the sort!" Keshef replied. "I doubt Nefertari even knows of my fondness for her..."

"Your fondness for her...but she called you nafis!"

Keshef frowned for a second, and then grinned widely.

"Well I know that, but that seems like a life-time ago now. She has really impressed me since we have been on this journey. She is bold, strong and her smile is so lovely..."

"Have you told her any of this?"

"Well, no," Keshef replied, "it is the Medjay way to ask a relative first, to inquire if she is be-trothed..."

"Betrothed!" Ahmesh cried. "She is only 12 years old!"

"It is not uncommon where I am from," Kes-hef retorted. "So she is not spoken for?"

Ahmesh mouthed the words "spoken for," shaking his head in amazement.

"Look Medjay: I'll not pledge my sister to be married to anyone, no matter how many cattle you give over. This she will decide for herself."

Both boys sat back in silence for a moment, until Ahmesh raised an eyebrow and leaned for-ward again.

"Just for my curiosity Medjay," the prince asked, "what sort of cattle are we talking about?"

"Why only the best," Keshef replied with a great smile. "The purest, most ancient of breeds - from the earliest times of our Kushau ances-tors!"

"Really!" Ahmesh whispered in astonishment, leaning closer.

"Indeed!" the Medjay went on. "Some bulls have horns that span wider than you are tall. The milk of our cows lets one join with the di-vine, helps develop the unseen eye and raises the neteru up like the tide inside you!"

"We have few left like that in Kemet," de-clared Keshef breathlessly. "kept at the most sacred of all temples..."

"You will have many more if the princess and I unite!" declared the Medjay boy proudly.

Ahmesh sat back in amazement, his respect for the Medjay multiplying at this great revela-tion. The mighty wandering Medjay still kept entire herds of the sacred cattle that helped start Kushau civilization! He contemplated how the arcane blood rituals of the Hyksos, which spread fear and confusion among the masses, could finally be offset by the sacred milk of such cows. But he shook his head again.

"Even if I agreed to this Medjay - which I do not," Ahmesh declared, "it would be our Mut who would have most to say in this matter..."

Keshef looked at Ahmesh, the smile fading from his face.

"I hate to remind you my friend, that it is likely that your Mut and my older brother did not survive the battle with the Kushna back at the boats. If he were here my brother would be having this conversation with you. But alas it is likely we are on our own."

Ahmesh sat back silently to contemplate the Medjay boy's grim reminder. Then he settled back to lay upon his sleeping blanket.

"I don't want to lose another family member so we had better get some rest Medjay. At dawn we find my sister."

The boys rose with the orb of Aten and got underway. The day was bright and the terrain arid, making the dry sandy footprints easy to follow. Before long they spotted Nefertari and Ten Na sprawled out on the side of a small hill.

"Nefertari!" shouted Ahmesh as they ran over to them. He palmed his sister's chest and was relieved to feel her beating heart. Then the prince gazed down at his sister's serene face, crying: "Sister speak to me!"

As the boys kneeled down to examine them closer, Keshef lifted Ten Na's head and looked at his mouth. Then he did the same to Nefertari. Looking around, he spotted the bush a few feet away.

"Fool's feast," said Keshef in a grim voice. "They have eaten it."

"What?" asked Ahmesh, cradling his sister in his arms. "What happened? Why won't they wake up?"

Keshef stood up. Shaking his head sadly, he pointed at the beautiful shrub.

"That plant is "fool's feast," a most tempting poison and they have eaten it. One or two berries can make you very sick and it seems they ate much more than that."

"What can we do?"

"I am afraid there is nothing we can do my friend," declared Keshef with great sadness. "There are remedies known among the most wise of my people, but I am afraid such knowledge is beyond me."

"But there must be something!" Ahmesh blurted. "We can't just leave her like this..."

Keshef sighed, looking off in the distance for a moment.

"We shall make them as comfortable as possible... until the end..."

Tears began streaming from Ahmesh's eyes as he hugged the limp body of his sister to his chest.

"How long do they have?" he sobbed.

"A day, perhaps two..." Keshef replied, holding back tears of his own. Then he put his hand on Ahmesh's shoulder. "I am sorry my friend. She would have made such a good wife..."

"P-Haaat!" Nefertai cried at the shadowy humanlike figure before her for the hundredth time. "P-Haat!"

The dark figure once again faded away and she was left alone again in what she knew was the spirit realm. Nefertari did not know how long she had been here, but remembered waking up in this place after falling atop Ten Na. Her Mut was a high priestess as well as queen, and had told Nefertari what the spirit world may look like. Given the circumstances, Nefertari concluded that this was it.

She sat on a soft couch similar to the royal furniture she knew back home in Kemet. But she knew she was not home because she was in a small, rectangular room made of multicolored curtains instead of walls. Outside the curtains strange white and grey lights swirled by and the floor seemed to be made of the same lights somehow solidified. Nefertari accepted that she was dead shortly after arriving, and had awaited a spirit guide or ancestor to come for her. Instead the shadowy figure had arrived, demanding to be let inside the curtain. By the low, dark vibrations emanating from the spirit like a fine mist, Nefertari recognized it as a Dark Deceased individual, a fallen spirit. So she had spoken the purification hekau to get rid of it.

"P-Haaat!"

Each time she spoke the word the being indeed faded away, but, like now, it only came back again. Wailing, protesting and speaking as if she knew her.

"Sister let me in!" the spirit roared as it flit back and forth outside the curtain. "I can send you back to your brother!"

Nefertari had heard it say that before and had always cut the spirit off before it said anything else. The princess had been told to never trust a word spoken by a Dark Deceased, and prepared to send it away again. But it blurted the next sentence quickly before she spoke the word:

"I can help you save your people Nefertari!"

The princess hesitated. Her lips were formed to speak the hekau, but instead she answered the spirit.

"What do you know of my people?" she asked.

"I know much," the spirit replied. And for the first time Nefertari could clearly make out that it was a female. "I know that they will never be saved if you die on this hill today."

"What are you talking about?" the princess replied, "I am already dead."

"No! You are not!" the spirit cried. "This is

merely a stopping point, a station on the way to the after world. Your brother awaits you in the world outside right now."

"Why should I believe you?"

"Why should you not?"

"Because you are Dark Deceased, a fallen one..."

"That is truth, but did not your Mut teach you that some fallen spirits are dark due to injustice," the spirit argued. "That is what happened to me. I am asking you to go back to the world of the living so that you can right this wrong. Then I can have peace."

"What is it you wish me to do?" Nefertari returned.

"Why, just save your people. That is all."

Nefertari thought for a moment. It seemed that this being was asking for help and she was taught by her Mut that helping the fallen ones was the right thing to do.

"You say that by saving my people I will also be helping you?"

"That is correct."

"Alright I will do it. But I ate poisoned berries, so I must be dying. How am I to remedy that?"

"Let me in and I shall show you..." the spirit said.

"But I can't get out myself," the princess cried. "So how am I to let you in..."

"Am I invited to come in?"

"Yes, but..."

"Then in I come!"

The shadowy figure came close to the curtain, and then stepped right through. As the spirit passed into the room it took on the form of a regal looking, dark skinned Kushite woman wearing ancient garb Nefertari had seen depicted on old monuments. Her breasts were bare, but a wide necklace of pure silver and gold slabs stitched together covered the top of them. A waist band of the same material held up a blood red skirt that touched her knees. Her feet were bare.

When the spirit materialized fully she looked around, giving the princess a view of her hair, which consisted of thick locks braided into a long tail down the middle of her back. Her eyes were black, with no whites showing at all. Her face seemed as if it had once been beautiful, but now had hard, harsh lines. This harshness, along with the eyes, told Nefertari exactly what type of spirit stood before her.

"A Set worshiper!" Nefertari gasped, stepping back fearfully.

The spirit nodded.

"It is true that I turned toward the ways of Set due to what happened to me," she replied. "But you can save me from that as well."

Nefertari relaxed a bit, but not much.

"You would turn away from the ways of Set if I help you?"

"Set brings nothing but grief. I want to go towards the light."

The princess relaxed a bit more.

"What comes next?"

"Come close," the spirit said.

Nefertari looked at the dreaded black eyes and hesitated. Her Mut had told her that those eyes marked the person as a high Set initiate. Such eyes marked a person as one who has surely drawn blood in the name of chaos.

"If I wanted to harm you I would have just let you die," the spirit cried. "Come here to me!"

Nefertari stepped forward and the spirit placed a hand upon her head. Immediately she saw strange images in her mind. The images had the quality of memories, but they were memories Nefertari never lived.

"In a former life I knew you," the spirit said, "You were powerful! You were the mistress of plants! You have the knowledge! Recall! Recall! Recall!"

Suddenly a flood of memories came back to

the princess about the plant world. The memories had no place in the life she was now leading, yet seemed to Nefertari as familiar as her own hand or foot. This was her knowledge and suddenly she knew plants to mix that would counteract the poisoned berries. In her mind's eye she saw plants growing near the hill of the poisonous bush, and knew exactly how to harvest them. Nefertari stepped back and looked at the woman spirit standing before her in amazement. The woman grinned.

I told you I knew you. And now you know more about yourself!"

"But what am I to do now?" Nefertari asked. "I'm stuck here. How can I get to the plants?"

The spirit smiled broadly.

"Ask your brother to do it."

"But...but how?"

"You are twins!" the spirit declared. "In olden times we practiced much magic with twins due to the great connections you possess. Concentrate princess and call out to him. Place yourself into his mind and you can show him what to do..."

"Are you sure?"

"Nothing is certain, but the bond between twins is notoriously keen. You must believe in your bond with him and concentrate. Then I shall teach you much more about yourself. We shall be friends."

Nefertari thought for a moment. Some of the memories released by the spirit were of a dark nature, indeed many of the plants she recalled were known to be used to harm, to put roots on people. She could not shake the feeling that the spirit was not being honest with her.

"No," the princess replied. "We cannot be friends..."

A look of panic suddenly came over the spirit's face.

"Nefertari, sister please don't send me back!"

"Thank you for helping me, but you are not

welcome here anymore."

"Nefertari no!" the spirit pleaded. "There is so much more I could show you!"

"I said no!" Nefertari shouted, pushing forth her hands in a shoving manner.

Suddenly the spirit dissipated, transforming back into a shadowy consistency. Then the shadow flew back and faded through the curtain. After a few more pleading words there came an especially anguished cry:

"We are sisters Nefertariiiiii!"

Then the spirit was gone.

The spirit's last scream unnerved Nefertari for some reason, but she decided to put it out of her mind to concentrate on her brother. Sitting on the couch, Nefertari closed her eyes and thought of Ahmesh. Suddenly several occurrences came to mind, like the time she had sneaked into the sacred pool for a forbidden swim and hit her head. She had told no one, and was sure everyone in the palace was asleep. But before she drowned somehow Ahmesh was there, pulling her out. Another was an early memory of her and Ahmesh as toddler babies. Ahmesh had disappeared from their playroom when their minder became momentarily distracted. Nefertari could barely speak, could not even walk, but somehow she had known her brother was in trouble and went after him. Just as Ahmesh was about to tumble down a long flight of stone cut stairs chasing a ball he was playing with, Nefertari crawled over and yanked him back by his diaper. The minder had found them both wailing a moment later and it had taken much effort to pry Nefertari's arms from around brother.

These memories informed the princess that no matter how many lies the Dark Deceased spirit had spoken, the bond between she and her twin brother was the truth. Keeping that in mind, Nefertari concentrated and spoke his name:

"Ahmesh!" she cried with all her heart.

Princess Nefertari

"Brother, it is me, Nefertari!"

Ahmesh snapped upright from his sleep, his sister's voice somehow ringing in his head. Suddenly images of plants started to stream into his mind in a jumble. His breathing became loud and excited, bringing Keshef, who was on final watch, running over to him.

"Are you alright my friend?" Keshef asked with concern. "Nightmares?"

"No!" Ahmesh declared. "It is Nefertari..."

Keshef took a breath, then walked over to Nefertari's still form and touched her neck.

"She is still with us my friend," he said. "So it could not have been her spirit..."

"Not her spirit..." Ahmesh cried, "her!"

Keshef looked back and forth at the siblings, then noted Aten raising on the horizon. He then went back and sat down in front of his friend.

"What is she saying?"

"She is showing me things," Ahmesh replied. "Plants..."

"What sort of plant?"

"Roots and leaves..."

Then Ahmesh got up and walked a short distance. He kneeled down in front of a leafy green plant with spikey leaves. Unclipping his sickle sword, he dug into the ground underneath it until he uncovered its roots. He hacked a large piece off and pulled it from the ground. Then he looked around the area again.

"What are you doing my friend?" asked Keshef.

"She is...showing me," Ahmesh declared as he disappeared around the side of the hill.

Chapter 4: He Said You Have A Lovely Smile

Keshef did not understand, but if this activity somehow gave Ahmesh comfort in dealing with the plight of his sister, he decided he would not interfere. Besides, the little Medjay had much to deal with himself, since he considered what happened to be his fault. Though they had needed food, it was his prideful rivalry with Ahmesh that led him to go on that hunt. It had been his pride, and, he now admitted to himself, his thirst to impress Nefertari, his secret love.

He walked over to the princess and Ten Na. Both lay still, struck down due to the poison of the berries. He nudged Ten Na's face with his foot. Somehow he knew the Kushna had led her to the bush, but it was his fault for leaving the princess alone with him. He had never left either twin alone with the wily Kushna, and if he had stayed he knew he would have prevented this. Then his precious Nefertari would still be here for him to win her as his bride. Now, the little Medjay prince concluded sadly, it could never be so.

As Keshef stood staring down at the still form of the princess, her brother came bounding back into the camp.

"I have it!" he cried. "I have the remedy!"

"What are you saying my friend?" cried Keshef, scampering over to meet him.

Ahmesh deposited two handfuls of roots and leaves onto his bedding, then reached into their cooking bag and took out the clay pot they used for heating water and a wooden cutting board. He shoved the cutting board towards Keshef, along with several of the roots.

"Chop these up fine my friend..."

"But are you sure about this Ahmesh?" Keshef asked. "Are you sure it was not just a dream."

"Are you sure my sister is going to die?" he

retorted.

"Unfortunately, I am," Keshef answered.

"Then what difference does it make to try this?"

"None, I suppose..." the Medjay prince replied.

Ahmesh nudged the cutting board closer to Keshef.

"Then please help me!"

Without another word, Keshef took out a razor sharp Medjay dart and cut up the roots. As he did this Ahmesh ground up the leaves he had collected with a rock, creating a short of paste. He then took the roots, along with the paste, and put them into the pot along with some water. Ahmesh then placed his hand over the top of the pot and shook it vigorously for a long while. He looked inside, shook his head and handed it to Keshef. Then the Medjay boy shook it for a while before handing it back. After nearly an hour of shaking back and forth, Ahmesh stuck his finger inside the pot and brought it out coated with a thick greenish yellow paste.

"It is ready!" he declared, holding his finger up high.

Ahmesh kneeled over his sister and began applying the paste to her upper lip, to her chest, temples underarms and to the back of her hands. They waited a few minutes, and then her eyelids began to flutter. Moments later the princess began to shake violently.

"Hold her!" ordered Ahmesh as Keshef seized the princess.

After a few moments the shaking began to cease, then her eyes and mouth opened. Ahmesh could see her swollen purple tongue and poured some of the remedy into her mouth. After swallowing it, his sister gave him a weak smile and held his hand tightly.

"You are going to be alright now sister," declared Ahmesh.

Keshef did not understand what had taken place, but he was beaming with joy as he looked down upon Nefertari. That is until Ahmesh added:

"Both of you are going to be fine."

"What?!!" howled Keshef in anger. "It was the Kushna who led her to that bush, I am sure of it! Why not leave him to his fate?"

"That's not the way of Kemet my friend..." replied Ahmesh.

"Well I don't care!" cried Keshef. "He nearly killed my...he nearly killed Nefertari and I won't stand for him anymore!"

Keshef then pulled out a Medjay throwing dart.

"I'll cut his throat! Your remedy can't cure that!"

As the Medjay prince tried to pull away to do the deed, Nefertari grasped him by his hand. Keshef looked down at her and she shook her head. He thought first to pull away, but, thinking that may hurt Nefertari, he just froze in place. After looking into her eyes for a long time, he put the dart back and the princess let go. As Ahmesh went over and started applying the remedy to the Kushna, Keshef got up and stomped off to the other side of the hill. It took much longer for Ahmesh to work on Ten Na due to his large size, so long moments later when a much calmer Keshef returned he was still working on him.

"I do not know what is wrong," Ahmesh said to Nefertari and Keshef. "His body shook, but he still has not awakened. Perhaps you don't need to kill him Keshef."

Nefertari observed with concern as Keshef walked over and looked down at Ten Na.

"If this is his fate, then good riddance," he declared.

The boys sat near Nefertari and gave her water. Then they cooked the other hare and ate it together. Hours went by without a stir from the still form of their Kushna prisoner. Near evening Nefertari needed help getting over to a stand of bushes to relieve herself. So the boys helped her over to it, and then waited for the princess to come back out. When they came back the Kushna was gone.

"Oh no," groaned Nefertari.

"I knew it," cried Keshef. "I'll go after him and finish this."

"No Medjay," said Ahmesh. "it is nearly dark. We must watch over Nefertari."

"But he is out there waiting to attack us!" cried Keshef.

"He must be as weak as I am," said Nefertari. "he won't be attacking anyone. We shall find him in the morning."

In the morning they tracked Ten Na until his footprints led to the highway. It was far too dangerous to follow him upon it so the decision was made to take to the hills again and get to the fort. According to Keshef it was only a day or so away. From there they could get well armed Kemetic scouts to come out and find the Kushna fugitive. So the children set off back into the hill country for the final trek to their destination.

On the morning of the second day they at last saw it. Though miles away, the huge walls of the fort loomed over the sandy landscape like a small man-made mountain. It was the largest structure Keshef had ever seen and he could not believe the twins when they told him there were even larger structures in Kemet. They had no choice now but to travel the road, because there was only sandy flat land between hills they descended from and the fort.

After several hours they spotted a wagon up ahead. It was standing still and the two donkeys attached to it were fidgety. Approaching cautiously, the children noticed three bodies lying nearby.

The dead men were long haired, bronze skinned, bearded sand dwellers and had a rough, hardened and hungry look about them. Two of the men wore chain mail shirts and still grasped shield and sword, while the other corpse's hands were empty, his mail shirt gone. Keshef stooped down and examined them closely.

"Recently killed," he declared. "Very recently, but the killers may be long gone now..."

"Oh, no I'm not!" a familiar voice shouted.

Up from the carriage of the wagon popped Ten Na. He wore the dead man's chain mail shirt and brandished his sword and shield. He sneered at Keshef, and then smiled evilly at Nefertari.

"You know you should thank me!" Ten Na declared. "These men were not only bandits, but cannibals. They scouted you out hours ago and actually intended to eat you. There's an entire band of them on the way and they planned to share you like roasted hares. It is time to come with me now Nefertari."

"She is not going anywhere with you!" shouted Ahmesh.

"Oh and I suppose you will be stopping me little prince," replied the Kushna humorously.

"I will stop you!" Keshef said, picking up a sword and shield.

Ten Na threw his head back and laughed heartily.

"Haa ha ha ha ha!" he guffawed, "Put all three of you together and you still would not outweigh me. I am a Kushna warlord and I have killed more men than the years of all your lives combined!"

Nefertari pulled her own dagger.

"We don't care!" she cried. "We have not come all this way to be stopped by you!"

Suddenly a Medjay dart appeared in Ten Na's

leg and he groaned in pain. Then another one sunk into his shoulder. He got his shield up just in time to deflect the dart that would have been buried in his throat, then the Kushna pulled the blade from his shoulder and tossed it away. Ignoring the blood flowing down his leg, Ten Na roared and leapt off the wagon, swinging his blade at the Medjay boy. But Keshef was too fast and pivoted away.

Ten Na, hatred blazing in his one good eye, kept coming, swinging viciously. Several blows glanced off the shield the Medjay prince wielded as the boy poked and prodded back at his much larger opponent. But Ten Na's sword work was seasoned, and it was clear that Keshef's shield was too heavy. Blow after blow, the Kushna began wearing him down.

So focused was Ten Na on battering away at the Medjay boy, he failed to immediately notice Ahmesh sneaking up on him. But the warlord was a combat veteran, and as Ahmesh leaped high, swinging his razor sharp sickle sword for his neck, the Kushna's swiveled. The blow intended to decapitate him instead dug a bloody furrow across the top of Ten Na's shoulder.

Howling in pain, Ten Na swung around leading with his shield, savagely slamming into Ahmesh. The little prince sailed 10 feet away, slid a few inches, and lay still were he landed. Nefertari glanced at her unconscious brother in shocked despair. Grinding her teeth, she fought back the urge to run to him, and then lunged after his attacker with her dagger. Stabbing low, she attempted to hamstring Ten Na so that Keshef could finish him off. But the warlord batted her dagger back with his much larger sword and then kicked her in the stomach. All the air gushed from her lungs, and Nefertari saw stars as she bounced across the ground. When her vision cleared she saw Ten Na battering Keshef nearly to the ground beneath the shield he held feebly above him. The Kushna then kicked the Medjay boy hard, causing sword and shield to fly from his little hands. Then, tossing aside his own shield, Ten Na seized the dazed Keshef by his locks.

Laughing in triumph, the Kushna raised his sword for the death blow.

Nefertari looked on in hopeless despair at Keshef, the smallest, yet bravest of them all. He was hanging limply by his hair, barely conscious in the hands of this monstrous man, giving up his life because of her. All because of her! Tears welled up in her eyes as she remembered how badly she had treated Keshef when they first met.

"If you kill him I go next!" shouted Nefertari.

Ten Na hesitated and looked back over his shoulder. There he saw his prize with the tip of her own dagger pressed against her belly. But the Kushna looked down at his hated enemy and only raised his sword higher.

"Surely you jest, girl." he replied.

Nefertari, tears streaming down her little dark face, pressed the dagger just past the surface of the skin of her little brown stomach. She winced as a thick trickle of blood flowed down to her skirt.

"No. I do not jest. If you kill my friend you shall go home empty handed because I shall fall upon this blade. Spare him, and I will go with you."

"I heard you all talk about meeting this Medjay during our journey," Ten Na sneered doubtfully, "you don't even like this boy princess..."

"Well...," Nefertari sobbed softly. "I like him now...I like him very much..."

"Enough to follow him into death?" Ten Na asked.

"Yes!" the princess shouted with conviction.

Ten Na took a long look into Nefertari's weeping eyes and what he saw there completely surprised him.

"You love this boy, don't you?"

Nefertari nodded, and then twisted the knife so that a little more blood flowed down her belly.

Ten Na then let go and the little warrior fell to the ground. As the Kushna warlord began walking towards the princess, Keshef rolled over and began crawling towards his sword.

"No Keshef!" cried Nefertari. "You are too hurt to fight! You will only get yourself killed! We can't beat him so I am going to go with him."

Keshef tried to raise himself up, but fell back weakly to the ground.

"N...no..." he cried with a pained moan.

"This is the way it has to be," Nefertari declared, "the only way. Take care of Ahmesh and get him to the fort..."

Ten Na came close and Nefertari handed him her dagger.

"I am glad you came to your senses girl..."

Ten Na took out a small rope and turned Nefertari around to tie her hands behind her back.

"Just like you Ten Na, I will attempt to get away every chance I get!" declared the princess.

"I would expect nothing less, princess," Ten Na chuckled.

Nefertari raised her foot.

"Starting now!"

Her heel came down and the Medjay blade embedded in the side of her sandal came down too. Nefertari could feel the razor sharp flint blade slice right through 3 or 4 of Ten Na's toe bones. Ten Na could feel it too because he dropped the rope and grabbed his foot, howling like a butchered animal. His cry of anguish was so loud that it woke Ahmesh up many feet away. Nefertari stepped away as Ten Na plopped down to see to his profusely bleeding foot.

"I will get you for this girl," he screamed in anguish. "I'll beat you senseless! And I'm going to kill that Medjay boy just as soon as I stop this bleeding. In fact - I'm going to kill both of them!"

"No. You will not," declared Nefertari in a matter of fact tone. "You won't be hurting anyone!"

Ten Na looked up from his bleeding foot just in time to see a large stone in Nefertari's hands come bashing down atop his head. When he came to a while later he saw Nefertari and the boys in the wagon leaving. He found that he was laid out on the ground, bound hand and foot and tied to the bodies of the bandits he had killed.

"I'm glad you woke up in time for us to say goodbye Ten Na," Nefertari shouted back to him over the clip clop of the donkey's hooves. "We've given up on taking you to the fort because you'll only try to hurt us again. So we left you to your new friends."

"These dead men?" the Kushna cried.

"Not them," Keshef shouted just before they moved out of earshot. "your new living friends. The ones who are coming right now..."

Ten Na looked the other way and he saw a band of twelve or so warriors walking towards him. Most wore mailed shirts and carried shields of the same design as the men he had killed. The warlord was filled with fear, but was sure he could talk his way out of being killed and eaten. These men were likely simple minded, he reasoned, so perhaps he could even enlist them to help get Nefertari back. As the men got closer, even after he saw how fierce and wild they looked, Ten Na still held out hope. Even when the men stopped to read something etched on the ground, glancing over at him angrily as they read it, the Kushna still had confidence. When they started a large fire, got out a large pot and began sharpening huge bladed axes, the

Kushna still thought his cunning would carry him through. But then they dragged Ten Na over toward those axes, pausing near the etched earth just long enough to show him the message that finally crushed his hope. The note read:

"This man killed your friends. Don't let him lie his way out of it."

Signed Nefertari, Princess of Kemet.

As Nefertari drove the wagon as fast as she could away from Ten Na and whatever fate was meted out to him, she kept a sharp eye out for more bandits. Though they both were in good spirits, Ahmesh and Keshef were injured and would be little help in case of another attack. Keshef's arm was likely broken, while Ahmesh could not get the ringing to cease in his ears. Both boys sat back in the wagon nursing injuries as Nefertari drove on, each jolt of uneven road causing more pain to their battered little bodies. Keshef's moans sounded especially mournful and she tried to assure him that help would soon be given at the fort.

"The only consolation I need is for you to consider being my bride," Keshef groaned.

Nefertari nearly fell over as she glanced back at the Medjay boy.

"Keshef you must be mad from pain," she replied. "Just try to get some rest..."

"No, Nefertari, he is serious," cried Ahmesh, "he said you have a lovely smile...and he has even offered cattle..."

"Nefertari," declared Keshef, "when I first met you I thought you were the worst girl I had ever met, but it turns out you are the best. I have much for your family if you will be my wife."

Blushing, Nefertari kept facing forward so that the boys would not see her smiling

"I...well I..." she stumbled.

"Well...yes?" asked Keshef.

"Keshef," said Nefertari carefully, "you have

become very special to me. I admit to having developed...certain feelings for you. But let us just get you some help first, alright?"

"Alright...but if you say yes now it will help relieve the pain!" Keshef moaned, causing the princess to laugh and shake her head.

After a short while the fort was near enough for some of the sharp eyed lookouts to spot them, causing much activity along the wall. Soon they got within shouting distance of the huge building, which was 6 or 7 stories high and made of massive blocks of red mud brick. But they found they did not have to shout because the huge, two story high wooden doors slowly creaked open. Out walked forty or so Kemetic troops, bristling with armament for war. They marched right up to the wagon and circled it. Then a tall warrior wearing formal Medjay garb stepped forth from their ranks, his purple cloak and headband supporting two feathers marking him as a high official. He walked right up to the wagon, looked them over and bowed.

"Hail and greetings royal children," the man said with a large smile. "we have been expecting you!"

"Hail and greetings viceroy Ahjay," prince Keshef greeted the man in return.

"Hail and greetings viceroy Ahjay," declared Nefertari and Ahmesh as one.

"Come," Ahjay replied, beckoning Nefertari to drive the donkeys forward. "Your families wait."

All three children looked at each other, wondering just what the viceroy meant. In short order his meaning was revealed as the huge doors of the fort closed behind them and they found themselves surrounded by many more warriors and officials from both the Medjay and Kemet. There were hundreds of them and they made a lane with cheering throngs on either side.

Nefertari drove the wagon right up to a raised platform that supported two thrones. Seated on the thrones were a broadly smiling Queen Ah Hetep and Prince Pakhu of the Medjay.

Having feared that they would never see them again, Nefertari and the two boys sat for a moment in open mouthed astonishment. Then tears came pouring from their eyes as both royal officials stood, opening their arms wide. Nefertari leapt down from the wagon and ran to her Mut's arms, while Ahmesh and Keshef were assisted by several of the warriors and carried over.

"The oracles informed us that this was to be your rite of passage," declared Queen Ah Hetep as she crushed the twins to her breasts. "That is why we did not sent you help. It is so good to see you my children!"

"I knew you would do it," Prince Pakhu declared as he carefully embraced his injured little brother. "You are a true warrior worthy of song and praise Keshef."

"Thank you brother," Keshef said, nodding toward Ahmesh and Nefertari. "and so are they."

As the cheering continued, Queen Ah Hetep and Prince Pakhu stood facing the crowd, placing the children between them as they soaked up the adulation. Nefertari and Keshef found themselves standing right against one another and almost instinctively their little hands came together. With their arms slightly behind them, so no one could see their tenderly intertwined fingers. Nefertari leaned over and spoke into Keshef's ear.

"As I told you on the ride here Keshef," Nefertari said, "I have a great fondness for you too. But I am not ready to be betrothed just yet. Come back in a few years."

A flash of disappointment came across Keshef's face for one small instant. Then he smiled and leaned close to Nefertari's ear.

"Fair enough then," he replied. "just promise you

won't consider another offer without letting me have my say again..."

"Fair enough then," Nefertari agreed with a nod. "You did save us after all, and you have a lovely smile too."

Keshef beamed that smile at the crowd, as Ahmesh and Nefertari smiled also. Then drums began to beat and a Ritual of Return began in honor of the impossible journey of the brave royal children.

MEDJAY WARRIORS

Chapter 5: Our Guests From Hattusa

The tall brown skinned warrior stumbled weakly down the long palace hallway, as sounds of the fierce stick fight he had just fled away from rang out behind him. Sharp stick to stick pounding followed by the stick fighter's battle cry of "Huh!" with each blow signaled to all within earshot that another fierce practice session was at hand. And the female voice crying "Huh" louder than all the others informed any listeners about the identity of its instigator. The warrior staggered to the end of the hallway, where he practically fell into the arms of the two guards assigned to this section of the royal palace.

"It is her again?" asked one of the guards as they stood the bruised and exhausted warrior up.

"It is," he replied breathlessly. "You must get Master Tu Ka Na…"

"He is on an errand," the second guard answered. "not to return until the morrow."

"Then for the peace of Ausar go and get the prince!" cried the stick fighter.

The first man nodded and hustled away, as his companion helped the stick fighter to a chair. Tugging loose a lightly tied flask from his waist, the guard gave the distraught man some water and they waited. A few minutes later the other guard returned with prince Ahmesh. The tall, wide shouldered royal, renowned for being the very image of his grandpa Shekem Sekenen Ra Ahmesh The Mighty, stopped and stood over the seated stick fighter with his fists on his hips.

"What happened to you?" he asked in his powerful, deep voice.

"Sire, your sister, the princess happened…"

"I told you and the others not to practice with her anymore!" roared the prince shaking his finger in the man's face.

"But then she tells us we have to!" cried the poor stick fighter. "And when we insist on obeying you she claims the right of first born, saying we have to do as she commands..."

Ahmesh sighed, shaking his head.

"Ah, that again..."he replied. "I shall speak to her now. Are you seriously hurt?"

"Mostly my pride, sire," the man replied. "But please stop her before she does hurt someone..."

As Ahmesh turned and strode down the hallway, the stick fighter cried:

"She does not fight fair sire! Nor does she fight like a female!"

"That's Tehuti's truth atef," agreed the prince with a head nod. "Tehuti's spoken truth."

When he pushed the door open to the battle practice room, prince Ahmesh immediately saw several other men on the floor groaning. None seemed seriously hurt, but all were bleeding and battered. Across the room he spied Nefertari. Twirling her stick fluidly, she looked every bit the proud, tall and strong Kemetian princess she was renowned to be. Her long braids wrapped in a tight cloth, Nerfertari wore the traditional stick fighting garb consisting of a cushioned shirt, leather skirt and cloth wrapped knees and elbows. Perspiration glistening from her dark brown skin as she wielded her stick expertly, squaring off against two male fighters who circled her warily. Nefertari taunted one about his lack of manliness, causing him to charge in with an overhead swing as she swiveled, holding her stick close to her torso. When the strike swished past she jabbed the warrior in his exposed rib cage twice, fast as a cobra, with the butt of her stick. As he fell over in pain Nefertari booted him aside, then the other warrior took a step forward to engage her.

"Stop!" cried Ahmesh.

The man hesitated, glanced back and realized who addressed him and stood at attention. Ahmesh was, after all, commander of the Kemetic army and no warrior dared defy him. Nefertari looked over at the prince, rolled her eyes, and then locked gazes with her opponent.

"Keep going atef," she said to the warrior.

"You heard me atef," cried Ahmesh pointing at him, "stop now!"

"And you heard me!" Nefertari growled at the fearful and confused stick fighter.

The man looked back and forth at both prince and princess several times, and then he threw down his stick and ran from the room.

"The rest of you follow him!" Ahmesh shouted, whirling his hand in gesture of clearing in the air.

As the other stick fighters got up and limped away, the prince approached his sister.

"Nefertari, we need to talk..."

"No we do not," she replied. "You refuse to practice with me. Elder Tu Ka Na is too old to practice with me. So this is what I have to do..."

"Mut says that you can hardly keep up with your spiritual studies because you sear your womb with all this heated battle practice." Ahmesh replied. "As a woman it is your role to parlay with the divine, to fight in that manner and leave the physical fighting to men."

"What has that gotten us Ahmesh?" Nefertari snapped back. "Look to the north and those vile asiatics still dwell within our borders. Look to the south and the Kushna threaten us there. We need all the warriors we can get..."

Ahmesh's eyes widened as the determined look on his sister's face told him what she was getting at. Then he frowned.

"Out of the question sister!" the prince barked. "There is no way you are joining me on the battlefield!"

Nefertari stepped nose to chest with her brother. Undeterred, she looked up into his eyes.

"But I am as good as any of your finest! The ancient annals tell of many woman warriors Ahmesh! Some led armies like you!"

"But you won't be leading any army Nefertari!" Ahmesh cried.

"Well why not?" his sister demanded.

"Because that is not your role!" the prince shot back. "Listen, you know as well as I that prophesy points to our salvation coming from the role of spiritual women. Great priestesses shall be Kemet's salvation! That is why Mut is strengthening the Priestesses of Amen. You are being groomed for that sacred task!"

"But what if I don't want to be!" screamed Nefertari.

Ahmesh looked down at the scowling face of his sister, shocked for a long moment.

"I know you don't mean that Nefertari." He replied evenly. "I know you don't, so I won't tell Mut you said that. You'll come to realize one day. But it will be too late if you burn out your female organs, your very conduit to the spirit world, by all this harshness and battle. Don't you want children someday?"

Nefertari let the stick drop from her hands and it clattered to the floor.

"You know I do Ahmesh..." she replied. "You know I wish to carry forth our line..."

"Then do as Mut asks," Her brother replied, "put this thirst for battle aside and focus on your priesthood training. Speaking of children, Keshef sent word that he would see you again. He'd make strong offspring through you sister and I'd be proud of them."

"He sent word? When?" asked Nefertari, her demeanor lightening.

A day ago..."

Nefertari nodded.

"Right on time to the day," she said, smiling.

"Indeed, the very same day for the last eight years since Djahy," replied Ahmesh with a grin. "We all saw you carrying on at the state dinner last year. He has not even taken a first wife while he waits for you. So when are you going to give him his answer?"

"When I am ready Ahmesh," Nefertari declared. "not a minute sooner."

Ahmesh sighed.

"Alright sister," he replied. "Mut and I will leave it be then. That reminds me: Mut wishes to speak to you too."

"About what?"

"We are having guests. Something she wants you to organize," Ahmesh said with shrug. "She would see you as soon as possible."

Nefertari nodded, and then walked out the door. She strolled down the long torch-lit hallway past painted images of Herukhuti, the neter of war and aggressive industry. The hawk headed one was depicted in various activities like blacksmithing, hunting and the defeat of enemies during just warfare. Nefertari had spent most of her time since Djahy under his watchful eye in this section of the palace learning his ways. After returning from Djahy those long years ago, she was determined that no one would ever terrorize her and harm those she loved like Ten Na had done. To ensure that would never occur again she dedicated herself to becoming one with Herukhuti. Nefertari was proud of the warrior skills but there was a problem: she had skipped several moon cycles and it was harder to concentrate during her spiritual studies. Though the truth was hard for her to admit, the princess feared her Mut was correct - her divine matrilineality was being eroded.

The princess turned left into another hallway, leaving the utility section of the palace for the residential area. Back in her private quarters she dismissed the bevy of handmaidens that rushed towards her, then walked over to a small couch and lifted up a cushion. Glancing around again to ensure she was alone, the princess glided her hand along a seam until her fingers slipped into a carefully concealed opening. Gingerly she pulled out a small flask filled with greenish yellow liquid. Popping the cork on the flask, she drank a small amount, replaced it and put the pillow back. Nefertari nodded in satisfaction as the spicy liquid settled in her stomach, thinking about the second lesson she had learned during the trip to Djahy. Another lesson that demanded she take action. Her battle practice saw to it that she would never fear bullying again, while this mixed plant prophylactic, concocted from her strangely recalled plant knowledge, ensured she and her family could not be poisoned either. The final lesson was that someone from inside the palace had betrayed her, setting her up to be captured and sent to the Hyksos. That someone had never been discovered despite great effort by the Queen and Elder Tu Ka Na, who had barely survived serious injuries as a result of that treachery.

Temporarily setting aside her desire to discover her betrayer, Nefertari then cleaned up and changed into appropriate attire. She chose a middle thigh green dress draped by a long, sheer and regal gown of gold fringed yellow. After propping up her long braids with a matching yellow tie, the princess left the residential area of the palace and entered the state services section. This area teemed with people from all over the region. Most Kemetians were there to petition for land, water or resource rights that could only be granted by royal elders. Foreigners were either diplomats or traders who shuffled back and forth between the Hyksos controlled northern lands and the Waset controlled south ruled by her family.

Walking down the long hallway to the working offices of the queen, Nefertari was greeted dozens of times by all who came near. Always one to be cordial, it took the princess a while to greet them properly. Finally, after 20 minutes or

so, the princess came to the large doorway leading to her Mut's working chamber. There she was
embraced by the queen's personal servant Ka-Ma-
il, a copper skinned daughter of the Hyksos taken
many years before in a war raid. An orphan, Ka-
Ma-il was noticed for her intelligence and sent as
a slave to the royal court. When granted her freedom after 10 years of servitude, as the war repa-
rations protocol of Kemet dictates, she decided
to remain with the only family she could remember. From that time on she had been accepted as
a close cousin by Nefertari and Ahmesh, and as
a sharp minded, well paid assistant to Queen Ah
Hetep. After it was discovered that betrayal had
taken place in the royal court, suspicion immediately had fallen upon Ka-Ma-il due to her parent-
age, but oracles readings and close observance
proved her innocent. Nefertari was overjoyed at
the revelation of her blamelessness, because it
would have broken her heart to be betrayed by
her beloved adopted cousin.

"Good day princess," Ka-Ma-il cried, her smiling, copper skinned face as pretty as ever.

"Good day Ka-Ma-il!" replied Nefertari. "Please
inform Mut that I await her attention."

"I shall indeed princess," said Ka-Ma-il. Then
she leaned in close to Nefertari with a sly grin.
"just as soon as you tell me when I can start
planning the wedding. I know Keshef sent word
again..."

"Oh cousin, stop it," Nefertari replied, blushing, "When the time comes, if you promise to keep
your mouth shut, I shall make sure you are first to
know...even before Mut..."

Ka-Ma-il giggled and nodded.

"Agreed!" she replied, then disappeared behind
the large doors to inform the queen about her
daughter's presence.

As Nefertari stood outside the huge ebony
wooden doors, she heard murmurs behind her and
turned. There she saw a group of foreigners com-

ing her way, causing quite a commotion. They looked similar at first to sand dwelling asiatics, but had lighter, olive colored skin and an air of civility most dwellers of the eastern dunes lacked.

They were dressed in fabulous clothing of a vibrancy of color, sleekness and shine Nefertari had never seen. The men sported short, neatly cropped beards as opposed to the long scruffy chin hair she normally saw on sand dwelling men. And the women were elegant, their eyes gleaming with a freedom of mind that the sand dweller men never allowed. Their regal look was topped off by bone white ivory combs that supported lustrous straight hair put up in tidy buns. The strange looking group, which consisted of two women and three men, stopped right beside Nefertari and nodded. The princess nodded in return as the door opened and Ka-Ma-il beckoned them all in.

As they were led into the chambers, several servants hustled out of the way holding papyrus rolls and candles. There in the middle of the room sat Queen Mut Ah Hetep at a large table, poring over documents. When she saw Nefertari and the others come in she stood and smiled. Nefertari walked over to her Mut and they embraced.

"Good day daughter," the Queen said, then nodded at the strange guests, "let me introduce you to our guests from Hattusa."

The three men stepped forward first, as was introductory custom in all regions known by Kemet. Two of the men were clearly twins, Nefertari noticed.

"These two are Tarhum," the queen said, waving toward the two look-a-likes. "and Tarcum. And yes, they are twins like you and Ahmesh, but identical. I will leave it to you to discover who is who because I can't tell."

"Hail and greetings, princess Nefertari," said the twins in unison.

"And this is Ishtan, the leader of this talented group." The queen said, gesturing to the third, older and wiser looking man.

"Talented?" Nefertari inquired, intrigued. "What sort of talent?"

"Let me finish," said the queen with an impatient toss of her head. "This is Wurusem, dance planner and Paya, who creates costumes."

Both women bowed and greeted Nefertari.

"Actually, I create all of our clothing, my queen," said the shorter woman named Paya.

"Really?" Nefertari cried. "You created these beautiful garments? You must sit with me and tell me about this fabric!"

"It is called silk princess," replied Paya. "And I will be glad to tell you all about it after our performance..."

"What performance?" asked Nefertari, turning towards the queen.

"The performance you are tasked with assisting daughter," the queen said with a grin. "These are the most famous performers from Hattusa. They are here to give a private show for the court this very evening. If we like them we shall invite them to perform for the rest of Kemet."

Nefertari grinned widely, due to her great love of such entertainment.

"It will be my pleasure." the princess declared. "Come and let me show you the royal stage."

That evening the performance troop, called "Great of Hattusa" indeed lived up to their name. Ishtan and the other two men played drum, flute and harp for several moments to warm up. Then Paya and Wurusum put on an astonishing snake dance, using actual trained serpents wrapped around their bodies. Both danced topless, executing whirling leaps and sensual gyrations, wearing green skirts that matched the color of the large serpents that adorned them. At the climax of the dance, the Hattian twins joined the women for several rhythmic moments as Ishtan continued to drum, before finally sweeping them aloft and tossing them gracefully through the air. Upon landing the women faced the audience and clasped hands, undulating their bodies in a serpentine, rippling motion back and forth. This was obviously the signal for the snakes that adorned them, because the animals slithered down from the neck and shoulder of each woman to their waist and writhed there for a moment, making it seem as if their clothing had come alive. Then the snakes wound back upwards, heading for their extended arms. Wriggling across each other, they traversed the arms from one woman to the other, each wrapping around a still undulating torso. By this time the Hittite twins had ran back to their instruments and joined in for the finale. After a dramatic musical buildup, it ended as each exchanged snake writhed back into place across the dancer's necks, their scaly tails settling to rest on the very last note.

The royal court exploded with applause. Nefertari and Ahmesh, seated on either side of the queen, looked at each other with great joy. Tu Ka Na, Ka-Ma-il and the two dozen or so invited relatives and courtiers were equally impressed. Even the queen, who was rarely impressed by anything, clapped and smiled vigorously. Ah Hetep was indeed so impressed that she leaned over to whisper in Nefertari's ear.

"Control of such creatures is not possible without higher knowledge dear," she said as she leaned even closer to Nefertari. "You can learn to do much more if you would just give up all the fight training."

Nefertari nodded respectfully. She had gotten used to her Mut taking every advantage she could to prod her about her spiritual studies. So the princess took the jab in stride as she wondered about the nature of the higher knowledge

Princess Nefertari

they studied in Hattusa. As they continued to look on Ishtan got up from the drum to address the audience.

"We hope you have enjoyed our performance so far," he said to more enthusiastic clapping. "Now it is time to bring you a story that is dear to us. It is similar to your tale of Auset and her passion for her husband Ausar. But it is different and reflects the foundations of the people of Hattie. But we are short one player and would ask that the princess Nefertari join us for the role…"

Everyone looked at Nefertari as she sat back in surprise.

"Me?" the princess cried, "But friend Ishtan, I know nothing of the ways of your people…"

"You need not," replied Ishtan, "It is a simple role, that of Istustaya, our silent goddess of fate. It is fate that embraces us all and that is what she represents."

Nefertari looked around. Everyone smiled and nodded, eager to see her join in the performance.

"What would I have to do?" she asked.

"You will wear the mask of Istustaya and come forth at crucial moments to embrace the hero of the performance, Taru, god of thunder and storms. At times of great importance he is compelled to embrace his fate which is embodied by the goddess Istustaya."

Nefertari smiled and nodded, then left the royal table and joined them on the stage. Paya took her aside and, after rummaging through several great chest filled with performance props, gave her a beautiful and elaborate silver and lapis mask. The princess was then instructed to put it on and walk out with great flourish when signaled by Ishtan. As Taru, played by Tarhum faced times of trouble, she was to sweep him in her arms and hold him until he accepted his fate. Nefertari agreed, put the mask on and waited.

As the play unfolded it revealed the drama of Taru, god of thunder and Lelwani, his elder sibling and crippled god of the spirit underworld, portrayed by Tarcum. The underworld god walked with a cane and was reluctant to face his enemies in battle. He was depicted as a crippled weakling, afraid to lead his army in a war to save Hattusa because his only concern was for the spirit world. Taru, who adored his elder brother for bringing down the way for the people to contact the spirit world, was being petitioned by the masses to replace Lelwani and defeat the enemies of the people. But Taru knew that the only way to replace his beloved brother would be through murdering him. At each fork in the road, during the contemplation of this deed, Nefertari as Istustaya was called out to embrace Taru. Near the end of the play Taru accepted his fate and killed his brother Lelwani. Taru then substituted spiritual laws with military rule, transformed the land into a war machine, and defeated the enemies of Hattusa. The play ended with the people of Hattusa rejecting Lelwani's perceived weak spirituality and becoming feared conquerors symbolized by the masses joining Taru in embracing Istustaya.

Nefertari played the role well, but wondered if anyone else noticed how indeed similar the Tale Of Taru was to the Passion of Ausar, but with the heroic leads and the ultimate lesson reversed. The princess was taught to respect the religious beliefs of others, but somehow the play made her uneasy.

The audience loved the performance because it was well done with music, costume and great dramatic performances. Nefertari took a bow with the rest of Great Of Hattusa, but could not put it out of her mind that something was wrong. Even after the guests ended the performance for the day and joined the royal family at the banquet table, the princess still had a strange feeling of foreboding. They ate, drank and socialized with their charming guests, who informed the royal family that they might be able to arrange for Kemet to acquire the fabulous silk fabric. This distracted Nefertari from the increasingly bad feeling she was having, but only momentarily. Even after they ended the evening, as both guests and attendees settled to bed, Nefertari still could not shake the feeling that the play was a sign of something amiss. As the princess curled beneath her covers for the night, little did she realize the accuracy of her intuitions.

It was the voices that awakened Nefertari.

Not the paralysis that numbed all of her limbs and disabled her mouth. Not even the jostling or the pitch darkness of being trapped inside of something. It was the voices, those of the men and women of Great of Hattusa and another voice much more familiar.

"This way." the voice of Ka-Ma-il whispered intently. "Are you fools sure no one saw you go into the princess' chambers?"

"No one left alive," stated the voice of Ishtan. "You paid for the greatest assassins and smugglers in the region. We did our job."

"Yes, but you failed us last time," the voice of Ka-Ma-il declared.

"That was not our fault," hissed the voice of Paya. "You gave us the wrong information. The layout was not as you told us..."

"Mind Paya..." warned the voice of Ishtan.

"Let her keep going," the voice of Ka-Ma-il warned dangerously. "let her talk herself onto Set's alter! Though I wear the flesh of this child, do not forget with whom you are dealing with..."

"She meant no disrespect Great Lady," said the voice of one of the twins.

It was then that Nefertari realized four things: she was in one of the chests brought in by the performers being smuggled away from the palace.

The false troop had found a way to subdue her, and had taken lives to get her. And the being who sounded like Ka-Ma-il, exactly like Ka-Ma-il, was not her beloved cousin. The voice was unmistakably hers, that was for sure, but the Ka-Ma-il she knew would never betray her and never, ever threaten a life in the name of Set. As the being had stated, someone was wearing her cousin's flesh.

The container she was in was placed on some sort of platform, which the creaking wheels and donkey hooved indicated was a wagon. Nefertari struggled mightily to open her paralyzed mouth as she heard her kidnappers hail and pass the guards at the palace gate, but to no avail. After a few more moments she heard the familiar clinking of a bag of gold rings being caught by eager hands.

"There is half your pay." the voice of Ka-Ma-il said. "When you deliver her to Avaris you get the rest. Fail again and there is nowhere you can hide from us."

"Thank you, great lady." the voice of Ishtar said. "We will get her to Avaris, rest assured."

"The boat to take you north is waiting," the voice of Ka-Ma-il replied dismissively. "now, away with you."

As the wagon plodded on its course to the docks on the Nile, Nefertari listened carefully to the idle chatter of her kidnappers. She learned much, including the fact that "Great Of Hat-tusa" was a ruse the band had played on many people as they plied their trade of theft, kidnap-ping and assassinations across the region. The bandits were indeed from Hattusa, but were a group of condemned criminals wanted in many nations, not a talented performance troop. They talked of many things on the way to their wait-ing ship, including a great secret that Nefertari listened to quite carefully.

"Are you sure you applied enough of the elixir Wurusem?" asked Paya.

"It was enough," the voice of Wurusem replied. "I practically drenched the mask in it. She'll not wake up for a day or so."

"Ah, but it is ironic that a concoction from the homeland that banished us, made from common mushrooms and the delicious waro root, has given us so much success in our schemes!" cried the voice of Ishtan.

"Slightly aged waro root." the voice of Paya chimed in. "Do not forget I perfected the elixir. You fools had marks waking up left and right until I discovered that the aged root has the most potency..."

"Yes, yes you can have your credit," the voice of one of the twins added. "But it was our recipe, bequeathed from our dear Mut, who would brew it to put my brother and I to sleep, which began it all."

"Indeed," added the voice of the second twin.

Nefertari contemplated the banter she had just heard carefully. Obviously this elixir was something that had never failed them. But the fact that she was even conscious indicated that something had interfered with the process. Then the princess remembered taking her own elixir, which she concocted to fight against just this sort of occurrence. Somehow both concoctions were at war inside her, leaving her senses aware, but her body subdued. Nefertari thought long and hard on the journey to the docks, and as she felt herself being transferred over, then felt the rocking of a ship, came up with her only answer.

Concentrating on the deep meditational techniques taught to her by her Mut, she focused intently. At first the princess was frustrated because this was just the kind of awareness that she had been increasingly having trouble with as her warrior training had progressed. But then Nefertari thought of something: calming herself away from physical activity was the reason why she had not been able to focus, yet now she was totally unable to move externally. With that in mind, she took advantage of her paralysis, and it allowed her to focus more intently on stilling her mind and regulating her breathing than ever before.

Shutting out the banter of the bandits, Nefertari imagined herself to be smaller than anything she ever considered, then saw herself inserted inside her body. Flashes of light went by and suddenly Nefertari's consciousness was deep within, flowing inside the spirit lines surrounding her veins and organs. Looking around she could see the greenish yellow of her own concoction swirling around in a battle with another liquid that was reddish brown. The elixirs crashed against one another like giant waves of opposing seas. Then Nefertari noticed something else: when she concentrated on the reddish brown waves, they dominated and pushed back the greenish yellow. When she concentrated on the greenish yellow, the opposite happened.

With a cry of exultation, miniature Nefertari leaped atop the wave of greenish yellow liquid, riding it like a flying carpet. Reaching around herself, she scooped up gobs of her concoction, coating herself with it, becoming one with it. Then, with a mighty roar of determination, she pushed with her hands and dashed against the poison within her system. Bashing, crashing, bashing and more crashing, she battered the unwelcome elixir down. As she focused harder, the wave she rode grew larger, while the reddish brown wave that invaded her kept getting smaller and smaller. Long minutes went by, as Nefertari's spirit guided tides of her elixir to overwhelm the poison inside her body, until a final greenish yellow wave dashed against a puddle of reddish brown. But just as the princess was about to cry out for joy and triumph, she felt a presence near and turned around. There, riding the wave right next to her, was the dark deceased woman who had come to her years ago, in all her dark eyed, grim faced familiarity.

"You!" Nefertari cried. "What are you doing here?"

"Enjoying watching you rediscover yourself," the spirit replied. "I am quite proud of what I just witnessed."

"You don't have the right to be proud of anything about me." growled Nefertari. "You are not even supposed to be here..."

"I never left my sister..." the spirit said. "I have just been very quiet..."

"Well when I get back I will see my Mut," the princess shot back angrily. "She will do a ritual and get rid of you for good..."

"I know how powerful the queen is my sister," the spirit replied. "But before you banish me away from you, ask your Mut why she has not allowed you access to the knowledge of who you were before...

"I am not going to ask her anything," spat back Nefertari, "and stop calling me your sister..."

"But you are my sister." the spirit replied back with a grin. "Just ask her. Ask her to tell you who you were..."

"I have enough trouble to deal with right now!" Nefertari cried angrily as she took a swing at the spirit. Hitting only air, she howled in frustration: "Leave me alone!"

The spirit looked at the fist that Nefertari tried to hit her with and grinned.

"Very well, I go now," the dark deceased spirit said. "Just ask her!"

She looked on as the black eyed Kushite woman fizzled away. Then, with a mighty leap, miniature Nefertari left the realm of her spirit body and returned to the conscious world. Suddenly the princess found herself back in the darkness, but this time she could flex her fingers and move her legs. Nefertari felt around inside the chest for a moment, and smiled into the blackness as her hand grasped something familiar. It seems there were other items packed inside the chest besides a kidnapped princess. One of those items was a crippled god's cane, made of long, stout, good hard wood...

Chapter 6: The Hyksos Are Your People!

Nefertari scooted down slightly in the chest and drew the top of the cane up near her chin in a striking position. Since she came back from her healing trance there had been little noise so she assumed her kidnappers were resting. That could mean it would be hours until someone opened the chest to check on her and she could not take the chance of being taken into enemy territory. So she raised the cane and knocked slightly on the lid. After waiting several moments, she did it again.

"Here now is that coming from the chest?" the voice of Ishtan asked groggily. "I thought you said you got the dose right this time…"

"I did get it right." the voice of Paya answered indignantly. "The girl won't wake up anytime soon. Must be props rattling about. Tarcum, go check it out."

Nefertari heard an irritated groan, and then footsteps came close as she readied. The chest was unlocked, the lid pried open, Tarcum peered in and then wood hit his skull. He crumpled to the deck without a sound. Nefertari rose silently from the chest brandishing the cane like a sword. Looking around she saw Paya and Ishtan on their sleeping blankets. Eyes closed, they snuggled up to get back to slumbering. It seemed that a night of murder and kidnapping was tiring work, Nefertari reasoned, as she observed Warusum and the other twin nearby snoring. Looking back over her shoulder at the positioning of Aten, Nefertari concluded that it was late morning. A glance at the shore told her that they were still in waters controlled by her family. It would not be long before they crossed over into Hyksos territory though, she concluded, so she needed to make quick work of this.

Stalking over silently, Nefertari chose her

first target. As the princess loomed over Paya, the woman stirred and looked up. But Aten was beaming over Nefertari's shoulder and the Hattian could not see clearly. Partially covering her eyes, Paya peered at the blurry figure before her.

"Tarcum?" Paya said, her eyes squinting upwards into the mix of light and shadow.

Then hard wood was the only thing she saw clearly, as it smashed mercilessly into her face. As Paya fell back, her painful groan alerted Ishtan. Their leader obviously had some warrior experience, because though partly blinded also, he managed to toss a sharp dagger. But Nefertari simply swatted it aside as Ishtan cried out in alarm. Then the cane descended on his head, and he too fell back onto his blanket.

Warusum and the other twin were quickly rising, but as Tarhum stumbled to his feet a wooden blow to the groin brought him back down low. Then Nefertari shot a whirling kick to his chin, followed by a second cane strike that sent teeth sailing over the deck and into the river. The Hittite man fell like a chopped tree. Nefertari placed her foot upon his neck on the remote chance he'd try to rise.

Having assumed a low battle stance, Warusum held a dagger towards the princess defiantly. But the Hittite woman's face was filled with astonishment and fear. Nefertari pointed to the quivering man under her foot, whose head lay in a pool of teeth and blood.

"Give up or you get worse," threatened Nefertari, shoving the bloody butt of the cane into her final foe's face.

The Hittite woman's hands were shaking as she looked around at what Nefertari had done to her friends. She tossed the blade down at Nefertari's feet.

"Good." Nefertari said, carefully picking up the dagger. "Now you have another choice to make. I am going to tie you all up and if you are

Princess Nefertari

in any way uncooperative I shall lay you low. Will there be any trouble from you?"

"No your Highness," the Hittite woman replied, her head bowed meekly.

"Good," Nefertari said, as she finally took a good look around the small passenger ship.

No one else was on board except the captain and one rudder man standing on the high deck. Their slack jawed expressions indicated that they had witnessed the entire thing. Nefertari waved at them.

"Ho! Captain!" she cried. "Do you know who I am?"

"Indeed I do princess," he replied fearfully. "But I did not know what these people were up to. I certainly did not...Please have mercy upon my shipmate and I. Please spare my boat..."

Nefertari looked at the two men carefully.

"I believe you captain," she replied gently. "These people fooled the royal court. We have all been victims of their treachery. Send your man down to help me secure this lot and turn this ship around."

The captain shoved his shipmate down towards the princess and nodded respectfully.

"Yes princess! Right away!" he declared.

"And do it with speed captain," Nefertari said as she and the shipman began securing the bandits from Hattusa. "I need to get back home."

As they sailed into the port the boat had departed from when they took her, Nefertari noted a commotion on the dock. Warriors were running back and forth, searching every boat and questioning everyone. After hearing her name spoken, the princess realized they were searching for her. As they slid up to shore Nefertari was spotted, then 20 or so warriors stormed onto the small vessel, seizing her captives and shoving swords into the faces of the captain and his ship man.

"Let them go," Nefertari ordered, waving her hands at the crew. Then she gestured towards her bound kidnappers. "Just bring this lot along and get me back to the palace."

Nefertari walked into the throne-room holding a rope knotted around the necks of all of her pinioned kidnappers. She dragged them right up to the Queen, who sat forward apprehensively on her throne. Ahmesh stood to the right of her, while Elder Tu Ka Na and Ka-Ma-il were standing to the left. They all stood up to rush over and embrace her, but Nefertari was all business and pushed forth a palm to stop them. She then signaled to the palace guards and they shoved the Hattians down to their knees.

Nefertari still held the cane she had used to subdue them. Slapping it in her palms, she looked each of them in the eye. She then pointed the cane at the leader Ishtan.

"You shall tell the Queen Mut everything." she ordered. "Now Talk!"

"The Hyksos," Ishtan began, "they hired us to get the princess and bring her to Avarice."

Ahmesh had his hand upon his sickle sword, his eyes blazing with anger. He was about to pounce, but the queen grabbed his arm. Elder Tu Ka Na leaned over and whispered something to the queen. She smiled grimly, and then pulled Ahmesh over and spoke into his ear. Her son stepped forward. Pulling his curved blade, he pointed at the cane in Nefertari's hand. Realizing what they wanted, she tossed it at her brother and his sword moved nearly too fast for the eye to see. The cane clattered to the floor in four pieces as Ahmesh's blade spun back into its sheath.

The prisoner's eyes widened and their mouths dropped open. Nefertari had been sheer terror on the boat, but each Hattian thanked their gods it had been her instead of her brother. After giving them a moment to contemplate the deadly skill of her son, the queen addressed the Hattians. "You took a princess of Kemet, killed four guards and spat on the hospitality of the royal house. Tell me: Why should I not let my son do to you what he just did to that stick?"

"Because we will tell you everything," cried Paya fearfully, as the rest of the prisoners besides Ishtan nodded in agreement. "We know about their plans with the Kushna! We know everything!"

"What plans?" growled Ahmesh.

"Shut up Paya!" cried Ishtan. "You know what will happen if we..."

Suddenly Ishtan grabbed his chest, along with the rest of the Hattians. They all fell back to the floor, writhing and twisting as if their insides were being pulled out. Everyone looked on in shock, including Nefertari, until she spied Ka-Ma-il standing to the side of the throne. Her beloved cousin's eyes looked strange and her lips were moving. Nefertari had wanted to handle the issue of Ka-Ma-il's apparent possession in private, but now she had no choice. Pointing at Elder Tu Ka Na, she cried:

"It is Ka-Ma-il! She is possessed! Elder stop her!"

Elder Tu Ka Na turned toward Ka-Ma-il and nearly recoiled due to the hate filled coal black eyes that looked back at him.

"Hyksos witch!" he cried.

Elder Tu Ka Na tried to seize ahold of Ka-Ma-il, but she shoved him back with amazing strength and he fell to the floor. The being in possession of Ka-Ma-il then shouted toward the ceiling and what looked like a small thunderstorm appeared there. As thunder claps boomed and streaks of lightning zipped back and forth in the clouds, the small storm rushed down upon the writhing Hattians, settling over them. Screams of pain and terror arose from the clouds as the thunderclaps became so loud that everyone covered their ears. Nefertari, who had been knocked to the floor, looked up to see her Mut standing before her throne rigidly. The queen had her eyes closed and her mouth was moving. Suddenly the dark eyes possessing Ka-Ma-il grew wide as she was lifted up, spun horizontal with her face to the floor, and then slammed down hard. The Queen Mut had her hand out, controlling the power that had upended the being controlling Ka-Ma-il. As the witch tried to get up, the queen pressed down hard, until finally the body of Ka-Ma-il was still.

Suddenly the dark thunder cloud began to dissipate, but it was too late for the kidnappers from Hattusa. When the cloud blew away they were nothing but charred, smoking remains. The queen stumbled and Ahmesh was there to help her sit down. Tu Ka Na bent over the still form of Ka-Ma-il, examining her. He stood and nodded.

"She is merely stunned." He declared. "We must do something before the witch that rides her wakes up. She is too powerful, and I fear Ka-Ma-il would have to be killed..."

Nefertari stood over the smoldering remains of the fake performance troop. This was the first time she had been witness to the dread powers wielded by the witches that dwell among the Hyksos, and they were fearsome powers indeed. The dark deceased woman who kept visiting her had the same black eyes and the princess could not shake the feeling that she had some kind of connection to these terrible women. She had no idea what kind of connection, but Nefertari was determined to find out.

The queen rose and slapped her son's chest, letting him know she had regained her strength. Then she pointed to Ka-Ma-il.

"Bring her," she stated. "We go the House of Life. I'll not let the Hyksos have our Ka-Ma-il."

Two guards carried Ka-Ma-il through the palace, out into the private courtyard and up to the door of the sacred place of learning. Only a chosen few were allowed to enter, so Elder Tu Ka Na and Ahmesh had to take over and carry Ka-Ma-il into the House of Life. There were a few priests and students there, and all got up from their cushions to see what was going on. The queen waved them all away and they got the message that this was private business

They kept going past the areas where Nefertari usually received her instructions, which was a candle lit, incense filled, small room piled with papyrus books, meditation cushions and writing implements. In fact the family walked past all the areas on the first floor and went up the stairs that were forbidden to all but a few high priestesses and priests. Indeed these were the stairs the teacher's traversed to get texts from the fabled forbidden library. By getting the queen's permission to ascend these sacred stairs, Nefertari, Ahmesh and elder Tu Ka Na understood they were going to witness a new world of knowledge.

At the top of the stairs there was a landing area before a huge wooden door. Above the handle to open it there were seven latches. The queen walked over and pulled them all in a special sequence, causing the door to slowly creak open. She beckoned the family to follow and they walked into a huge library. Papyri were stacked on shelves that went almost to the very high ceiling. Ancient statues were everywhere and the walls were made of huge stones of the most ancient sort. Suddenly Nefertari perceived what she was looking at: Only the most ancient and holy buildings had giant blocks of stone of this sort, created in olden times by ancestors who dwelled as one with the creator. The structures surrounding this building were all built on a much smaller scale, which meant that the entire palace complex had been built around this sacred place of learning! Nefertari bowed her head and mouthed a silent "Tua Neter" to the creator for the chance to walk in this sacred place.

There were several small side rooms equipped with couches and they laid Ka-Ma-il out on one of them. Then the Queen Mut instructed Nefertari and Ahmesh to tie her cousin's hands and bind her feet and gag her. Queen Mut Ah Hetep then walked out into the library, coming back moments later with an ancient scroll.

"This is a text that explains how to deal with live possession," the queen explained. "Freeing a being of control by the living, instead of those exerting influence from the realm of the dead, is a difficult and delicate endeavor. You must help me to begin the ritual, and then watch over me as I wade into this battle. It may take as long as a day. I shall be in trance and you must keep me cool with water and fanning. Now join me in the hekau of this ritual.

The queen began reciting the sacred words and the rest of the family soon joined in. The being in possession of Ka-Ma-il woke up and began struggling, but to no avail. They had bound her well, so all she could do was glare with the black eyes of Set. After nearly an hour of chanting the hekau, the Queen Mut dismissed the family from the room. Gathering in the library, they decided that Nefertari would take the first watch. As the Ahmesh and Elder Tu Ka Na left, Nefertari settled down in a chair and looked around at the vast store of knowledge. Then it occurred to princess: Here was her chance to find the hekau that would allow her access to past life knowledge. She would see firsthand what the dark deceased woman was talking about.

After checking in on her Mut, who sat in silence on a meditation cushion beside the couch upon which they had deposited Ka-Ma-il, the princess came back into the library and began her search. Several hours went by and she began to see a pattern to the section dedicated to the hekau called "The Teachings of Transformations of RA." Nefertari had been taught that all things were possible through the interaction and manipulation of the holy spirit, the life force that pervades all, called RA by the people of Kemet. To access this power required the cultivation of the individual life force and the knowledge of the proper sound to manipulate it, called a heka.

After investigating the section devoted to Het Heru, the neter of sensuality and creativity, she found the heka she needed. But then Ahmesh appeared to take her place in the watch. They both walked into the side room and there saw Queen Mut Ah Hetep perspiring profusely. Ahmesh looked at his sister angrily and she rushed from the room to get water. Moments later Nefertari sprinkled the cool liquid upon her Muts head as Ahmesh cooled her with a large peacock feather fan.

"How could you let this happen Nefertari?" Ahmesh scolded. "Our Mut is in a battle to save Ka-Ma-il and all you had to do was watch over her!"

"I know brother and I am sorry." the princess apologized. "There is just so much knowledge here..."

"Oh I see," her brother replied. "you who forsook study suddenly wants to know it all. You can go - I shall take over from here."

Nefertari turned to leave, but before she got to the door Ahmesh called out. When she turned he threw the queen's royal robe to her.

"Give that to the servants," he declared, "Mut won't be needing it right now."

Nefertari nodded and walked out. She looked over her shoulder to make sure Ahmesh was not looking and walked over to the table where she had been studying. She snatched the papyrus containing the Het Heru hekau and stuffed it into the folds of the robe. Then Nefertari descended the sacred stair case, left the House of Life and walked back to her living quarters. There she unfurled the scroll and read it until she found the particular heka that allowed access to memories of past lives. After repeating it over and over, the princess sat upon a cushion, regulated her breathing and began to chant it inside her mind.

Over and over for hours she chanted the heka, until finally memories similar to those the dark deceased woman had shown her began to appear in her mind. Jumbled images crashed against jumbled images and for a while Nefertari could make no sense of it. Finally she saw a young girl, a little princess, hand in hand with another little girl who looked just like her – her twin! They were surrounded by a royal family. Nefertari could sense that this little girl was her in another time. As this child she felt great joy and enjoyed a childhood surrounded by love and caring, but there was something else more dominant in this life:

Fear.

The girl of this lifetime lived at a time when Kemet was pervaded by fear and uncertainty. Tumultuous images of warfare and a starving populace beating at the palace gates made Nefertari draw the conclusion that this was the time of the turmoil just before the Hyksos arrived. This was quickly confirmed when she heard people speak the name of he who sired her in this incarnation: Shekem Nehesy.

A kindly, yet weak king, Shekem Nehesy was infamous for making decisions that crippled Kemet. His unwise rule resulting in breaches of international treaties, disruption of trade routes and a porous border allowing all manner of people to seize Kemetic land and holdings. Nefertari saw she and her twin sister arguing with their pa, then storming out of the palace in anger. Next she saw the two sisters plotting to do what their pa could not: secure Kemet's greatness once again. They decided to do so by taming a strong barbarian sand dwelling nation and use them to subdue other tribes threatening Kemet. Their treacherous end game would be turning upon these pawns and destroying them later. So the sisters stole palace riches, hired mercenaries and traveled in secret to a sandy, eastern land past Djahy, where they met with tribal warlords.

Nefertari recognized these people as the primitive Hyksos, and her blood ran cold. Suddenly she realized who the sisters were. Suddenly the daughter of Queen Mut Ah Hetep wanted to turn away from the images streaming before her, because she knew where they were leading due to legends about this time and these people. But it was now too late. No one could save Nefertari from the terrible truth being displayed before her by the revelation of her past existence.

Next she relived the sister's fruitless attempts to teach higher spiritual knowledge to these wild eastern tribes to soften them for domination later by the Kemetic people. The Hyksos could not perceive the higher Ausarian teachings, but were fascinated by Set, the Kemetic neter of chaos and disruption. So the sisters made the fateful decision to use this fascination to influence them. Delving into forbidden Set knowledge themselves, the sisters used it to manipulate the Hyksos population. Always with the intention of getting back to the Ausarian way, the sisters used Set knowledge to mold the Hyksos into a terrible war machine that indeed fulfilled their intentions.

It took nearly a generation, but the barbarians that threatened Kemet were indeed destroyed by the mighty Hyksos nation forged by the sisters. But when they marched in as liberators of the land, with a vast army and a cadre of specially trained Set priestesses trained to spread terror and enforce their will, the two sisters had shed too much blood. Their will had become one with the neter of chaos and the Ausarian Tree of Life teachings of the ancients had been cast aside. Their eyes now permanently black, the sisters killed their own pa, usurped his throne and forsook the ways of Ausar forever. When the sisters died, in an ironic jest worthy of the neter of disruption himself, foreigners mounted their thrones. Set laughed as barbarians came to rule the northern land. And thus began unending warfare with Nefertari's current family of this lifetime, the strong natives who ruled the upper section of Kemet from Waset.

The princess did not want to believe it, but she both felt and remembered the story playing before her though the power of the past life heka. This was the life of the dreaded Great Betrayers she had heard whispered about all her life. Now Nefertari, to her ultimate despair, knew why her Mut was always careful about speaking about this time. Family discussions had always been hesitant about these times and especially about the black eyed Set-priestesses who tutored barbarians in forbidden knowledge that led to the killing, torture and sacrifice of countless innocents. The sickening images being displayed to the princess comprised the life story of these dreaded Great Betrayers. And now Nefertari knew, to her heart searing, gut wrenching chagrin, that she had been one of them.

The princess then opened her eyes, her body quaking with absolute dark despair. She had dug her fingernails into the palms of her hands as the revelation hit her, so blood flowed all over the couch she sat upon. But Nefertari didn't notice the pain, because no injury or torture could compare to the heart searing agony of the truth. Nefertari fell to the floor, sobbing uncontrollably as she remembered all the family members, uncles, aunts, grandparents, cousins and more that had died in the war with the Hyksos. And the babies! The most horrible rituals of the Hyksos involved the sacrifice of innocent children.

All of this, Nefertari thought with a shudder, absolutely all of it, was because of her. Then she

Princess Nefertari

heard the voice of the dark deceased woman again, adding to her guilt ridden agony:

"Yes they are all dead," the voice of the dark woman cried, "and yes it was because of you! It was because of us!"

"Get out of my head," Nefertari howled tearfully. "Leave me alone!"

"I can't leave you alone sister, especially now that you now know the truth!"

"What do you want from me?" asked Nefertari, screaming to the air around her.

"I want you to save your people sister! Your real people, the Hyksos! They are our children! We are their Mutu Nefertari! We gave birth to the Hyksos nation!"

On her knees now, as the words of her dead sister plunged like daggers into her heart, Nefertari tugged at her braids in bitter despair.

"No!" the princess cried in sobbing anguish, "Noooooooooooooooo!"

"Yes!" screamed back her dread sister. "The Hyksos are your people! Go to them! Go to them now!"

Nefertari ran over to a couch, seized a pillow and ripped it open. Out dropped her elixir and she popped the cork. She had to get the voice of her sister out of her head, no matter what. So she threw caution aside, pulled the vial of elixir to her mouth and drank all of it. Almost immediately her head started swimming and the voice of her sister was Muted.

"What are you doing sister," the voice in her head cried. "What are you..."

The voice disappeared just before Nefertari fell over into her bed, her consciousness failing. Sometime later, Nefertari did not perceive how long, the princess woke up. A servant was knocking on her door and Nefertari ordered her to bring food and inquired about the time. It was now early evening, the servant told her and the princess nodded. It was the correct time for her to do what she now considered her only choice. Pulling out a small travel bag, Nefertari packed it with plain clothing, some toilet items and a bag of gold rings. Then she carefully cut off her braids and donned the plainest clothing she possessed. Next she found the cheap, bulky braided wig she wore as a child while playing dress up and put it on. Then she stole away, heading for the rear section of the palace. Early evening was the time of day servants left via the rear door and court way. Now there were nearly two dozen of them; mostly young women about her age, heading to this exit. Nefertari, keeping her head down and face lowered beneath her wig, joined them. She walked past the guards, who were on alert only for those entering, and then took a look back at the place where she was bred and born. She never intended to come back. Not ever again, because the revelation about what she had done, even though it was in a past life, had changed things.

Nefertari could never again look into the faces of her family knowing the destruction wrought by the Hyksos was her fault. The guilt of it, the crushing weight of it, was too much to bear. So she put one foot in front of the other and fled the palace area, determined to leave it all behind forever. She would disappear; first into the teeming population of Kemet, and then to parts unknown. Traitors did not deserve to rule over those betrayed, she thought sadly. And none ever turned against their own as treacherously as she had, by giving birth to the Hyksos Set worshipers. So Nefertari wiped her final tears and strode forward, determined to make a new path. Whatever that path might be, the self-exiled daughter of Waset concluded, she would be a princess no more.

Chapter 7: I am As Bad As They Come

Nefertari tossed and turned in her sleeping blankets, covering her ears with her pillow though she knew it would do no good. She had not rested in three days due to the constant mental torture cruelly served up by her dread sister. When she tried to sleep the dark deceased being entered her dreams. When awake she heard whispers inside her head. Always it was the same message and it was starting to drive her mad.

"Go to our people, my sister! Go back to our children, the Hyksos!"

Having slipped away from Waset, Nefertari secured passage on a southbound passenger boat, ending up in Djeba, the city of neter Heru. Here she found an out of the way lodging establishment, one of many that catered to the teeming throngs on pilgrimage to the city of the sacred hawk. Nefertari planned next to take a caravan to some southern land far away. But the mental badgering by her dread sister was unceasing and constantly made her dwell on her history with the Hyksos. The stress of it all made travel impossible, subjecting Nefertari to perpetual exhaustion and to a constant splitting headache. While the memories being dredged up only added to the ever increasing pain, paralyzing Nefertari to the point of immobility.

Nefertari had considered going to the local priesthood for an Ausar ritual to be rid of her long deceased sibling, but she knew the priests would surely know her and alert the royal family. She considered getting ingredients to mix more elixir, which would probably rid her of the voice, but at the cost of impairing her further. Wine dulled Nefertari's spiritual connection somewhat though, so she found herself a frequent visitor at the local drinking establishment.

As Nefertari shoved the covers away and sat up in her rented bed, it was to the drinking house that she decided to go. She dressed and walked out into the warm late night air, met by a slight breeze blowing in off the Nile. The drinking establishment was right around the corner and she saw the regular cast of characters she recognized from her frequent visits standing around as usual.

One man she had always noted was watching her carefully from a sales shop across the street, where he perched like an owl upon a wine barrel. This night he finally decided to say something to her.

"Ho, weary woman," the man projected in a low voice, "I have something better than that!"

"Better that what?" Nefertari replied, about to enter the door to get her drink.

"Why, better than anything you can get in there," the man answered, pointing at the door Nefertari was about to enter.

"Not interested," she said, stepping for the entrance.

"I have root of white lotus!" the man declared. "It makes you forget all your troubles..."

Nefertari hesitated, her old instincts perking up. It was her family that had cracked down on the illegal trade of white lotus root, a very powerful mind altering plant. But Nefertari reminded herself that she was princess no more, that her head ached fiercely and she had a lot she needed to forget. Nefertari turned and walked over to the man.

As she got close to him, Nefertari noticed that he was a tall, dark person with the thin nose of a far southeast Kushite, perhaps even from the horn shaped area that jutted out into the Red Sea. His loose, puffy clothing and thin pointy beard marked him as one of the mountain folk of that area. No matter where his place of origin though, he had the shifty eyes and crafty demeanor common to those who plied an illegal trade.

"Does it truly work?" Nefertari asked. "Does it take away memories? Even for a while?"

"My dear," the overly polite salesman replied, stroking his pointy beard. "My stock will have you floating on a wave of pleasure, without a care at all in the world."

"How much?" she asked.

"How much do you require? One medium sized dried root is enough for two or three days of pleasure..."

Nefertari looked around, and then reached into a pouch on her waist, pulling forth a medium sized ring of gold.

"How much would this purchase?" she said, holding the ring before his face.

The man's shifty eyes widened and a great smile appeared.

"Why my dear, that would get you a moonly supply! You must have some really bad memories."

Nefertari handed the ring over and the man grabbed it greedily.

"You take this," she declared. "Give me one root tonight and bring the rest here tomorrow. It had better work as you say or I shall beat my payment back out of you..."

"My dear worry not," the man replied jovially, pulling a white root from his sleeve and handing it to her. "We shall do business with regularity."

Nefertari took the root back to her room, sat down upon her bed and just looked at it. The voice of her dread sister continued without letup, causing the evil images of her past life to flash past her mind's eye again. Finally, with a sigh of pure exhaustion, Nefertari lifted the root to her mouth, chewed into it and swallowed the juices.

"The white lotus won't save you from your fate Nefertari," the voice of her sister cried out inside her head. "just do as I say and return to our people: Do as I say and return to the Hyksos!"

Suddenly Nefertari felt a rush of euphoria, as if all the nerves in her body had been washed over by a magical wave of pleasure. The colors in the rooms became brighter and Nefertari marveled at them as her head bobbed up and down. The voice of her dread sister ceased as all memories of this life and the last floated away on a cloud of happiness. Nefertari chewed the rest of the root, and then lay back on her bed. All night her exhausted body went in and out of peaceful slumber. And when awake she felt as if she were floating. Like a bottle on a softly rolling sea, floating and bobbing and floating.

Nefertari returned to the white lotus seller the next day and picked up her moonly supply. She went through it in a week and then went back for more. For the rest of the moon Nefertari walked around in a haze as all of her troubles were forgotten, just as the lotus salesman had promised. After missing meals for several days and even failing to wash herself, Nefertari paid heed the salesman's warnings and halved her intake. This left her in a euphoric, yet functional state at all times and kept the memories and voices out of her head. One day while playing senet with the lotus seller, whose name was Bekele, Nefertari asked about the origin of his product.

"Why it comes from my homeland at the headwaters of the blue Nile," he replied. "It is the most beautiful land in the world."

"If it is so fine a place my friend, why are you here in this land?" inquired Nefertari skeptically.

"Alas," Bekele replied, shaking his head. "The

ways of my people are too simple for me. The misty mountains and cool waters are enchanting, but I wish to see the wider world."

"It sounds like the right place for me though," replied Nefertari. "Tell me more about your land."

For the better part of the day Bekele regaled her with the tales of his homeland Amhar. His people, called the Amharis, did indeed live good lives surrounded by mountain terrain that had made them virtually unconquerable. The hardy, abundant grains they cultivated with ease afforded them with rich trade and provided plentiful food for both men and cattle. And for those more daring, like Bekele, there was always the trade in white lotus, which grew like a weed in their cool mountain waters.

"I wish to go there," Nefertari announced. "I would visit Amhar, and if it is all that you say it is, I may just stay there.

Bekele regarded her for several moments, gazing at Nefertari over the senet board.

"You must be running from something terrible little sister," he said at last. "Very well, I am going back to resupply in a week. You can join the caravan but be prepared to pay. It will cost you one gold ring..."

"Fine," Nefertari replied. "I shall be ready at that time."

The caravan indeed left in one week and Nefertari was on it. Five large wagons, two owned by Bekele, left the city and took a famed road near the Red Sea. The popular route, called Sebek's Way due to the number of jackals seen along its path, was a neutral route for trade by all nations near it. No country dared attack travelers upon it, even during times of war, because nearby nations needed Sebek's Way, which passed through a series of well watered oasis, as an important route for trade.

Even with this unsigned treaty among nations in play though, the road could be dangerous due to freebooters, bandits and pirates. So they set out in the company of 25 armed mercenaries, charged with fighting off any threat to the caravan.

Nefertari was not very impressed after looking the hired men over. She expected half of them to run in the event of an attack, while the rest might put up a feeble fight. Most were too fat or to thin, almost all looked unhealthy. None, Nefertari surmised, would pass the inspection that her brother would put them through. But Nefertari did not contemplate safety issues for long because she was quickly introduced to a new level of mind altering joy. As she rode with Bekele, he shared with her some of his extra special golden lotus root. Nearly twice as powerful as the white, it took Nefertari to a higher plateau of blissful detachment as the journey got well underway. The world whirled around Nefertari as the days went on, because Bekele was extremely generous with the golden lotus. He never chewed it himself though, and had Nefertari been in her right senses, her natural wariness would have given her pause.

But there was no wariness, no suspicion. Only the root and its gifts of forgetfulness and pleasure mattered. After three weeks of traveling with Bekele on Sebek's Way, Nefertari would shake and feel sick within hours without it. She forgot about what she was there for, about where she was and even at times what her very own name was. Only the lotus root comforted her, and because Bekele supplied it, Nefertari's dulled senses told her he was her good and true friend.

However, four weeks into the journey the Amhari's real purpose was revealed, after the caravan rolled onto a small island of greenery amidst the sandy landscape. It was an oasis Bekele said marked the halfway point to their destination, and the place where he proved he was a friend to no one.

As the rest of the caravan disembarked for water and fruit, Nefertari cared nothing about where they were as she sat back in the covered wagon, head bobbing and eyes drooping. Concerned only about chewing her next lotus root, she failed to notice the two men who walked up to Bekele as he jumped down from his wagon. One was a short stocky Kushite, the other a bronze skinned Hyksos. Very well armed with daggers and shields, both looked battle hardened and dangerous.

"It is about time," the Kushite man said.

"We were beginning to think you had backed out," the Hyksos man added. "Which would have made us come look for you. And that would have been very bad for you Amhari."

Bekele unhooked his donkeys, handing the reins to another man from his caravan, who began leading the animals towards the nearby lake. Then he knocked some of the dust on his clothing, straightened out his shirt and walked toward the men.

"I'm here now." Bekele replied. "Have someone come get the goods. And take me to him."

The Kushite beckoned to a few men standing under the trees not far away and they approached Bekele's second wagon. As they began removing tied bundles of lotus, the Amhari followed the Hyksos warrior. Bekele was led to the far side of the small lake, where a dozen or so animal skin tents were set up. All the tents were simple brownish gold, the color of the antelope the hides were taken from. One tent though, twice the size of the others, and was painted with red and purple stripes. As Bekele got closer, he noted the symbol of the Medjay, two darts and a shield, painted on the cloth covering the entrance. It was this tent that Bekele was led into. The tent was well lit by several dozen candles. Twelve warriors stood at attention, six on either side of a large Kushite man sitting on a worn looking throne. Another warrior kneeled before the big man, his body quacking with fear. As the Hyksos man stepped forward to announce Bekele, the large man on the throne glanced up, and then held up his hand to halt them coming forward. All eyes were on the scared man as his sentence was pronounced.

"Everyone saw you run, Ha Beka," the big man announced gravely, "so to keep it from happening again, I'm taking five toes. You decide which foot you like best..."

"Nooo!" Ha Beka cried as several of the warriors grabbed him and dragged him past Bekele out of the tent.

The big man on the throne then shook his large, tightly braided head and beckoned them forward. He held out his hand and someone put a cup in it. By the time Bekele was announced someone had poured him a drink. As Bekele started speaking the man's big brown hand was pouring the drink down his big brown throat.

"Hail and greetings mighty Setja," declared Bekele with a low bow.

"I need neither your hail nor your greetings mountain man,"

growled Setja, wiping the back of his hand across his mouth. "What I do need is my lotus and you are late bringing it to me. And you shall address me as "Prince Setja" if you wish to keep your head."

"I am sorry Prince Setja," Bekele replied, shuffling slightly. "But I was delayed due to the acquisition of a gift for you."

The man sat back in his throne, a wide smile now beaming at Bekele.

Princess Nefertari

"A gift worthy of a prince?" he replied, raising an eyebrow.

"I do think so," answered Bekele with a smile of his own. "Allow me to go to the wagon and retrieve it..."

Setja waved his hand.

"Please do so." he replied.

Bekele walked back to the wagon. Stepping up on the pushboard, he peered in and saw Netertari sleeping. A half chewed lotus root was clutched in her fingers as she lay back breathing evenly. Bekele carefully leaned in and tapped the side of the wagon from the inside, which popped open a small compartment filled with three dozen or so golden lotus roots. He stuffed all the roots in a bag save one, tossed the bag over his shoulder, then slapped the root from Nefertari's hands and shook her awake. She groaned as her eyes opened, her empty fingers clutching at the air.

"My root," Nefertari moaned, "where is my root?"

"I have it here my dear," replied Bekele.

"Give it!" Nefertari whined.

"You can have it, but you must come with me," replied Bekele.

Holding forth the root, the Amhari got Nefertari to climb down out of the wagon. He grabbed her by the arm and they both walked back to Setja's tent. When they walked in Setja leaned forward, his eyes widening. He stood up as Bekele led Nefertari up right up to him.

"Ahh Amhari," said Setja with a smile, "you know what I like."

"Indeed prince..."

"She is even more beautiful than the last," Setja said with delight. "Her skin... like roasted nut from a palm. A Kemetic woman?"

"Most assuredly my friend..."

"High born, from the looks of her," Setja declared, looking Nefertari up and down.

"I would say so sire," Bekele replied. "Surely not bred from common folk..."

"Her family?" Setja asked.

"She claims not to have any, though I sense she is lying..." Bekele answered.

"Ahh, she is estranged..." Setja said, rubbing his chin with a satisfied grin. "A high born woman of quality stock, and no one will ever come looking..."

Bekele and Setja looked at each other, smiling evilly. The Amhari then handed the bag of golden lotus over to him, placing the single root in the hands of the weakly tottering Nefertari. Eyes glazed over, she bit into the golden stalk as both men watched.

That is it exactly, prince," replied Bekele slyly, "no one will ever come looking for her. No one knows where she has gone. Keep her on the root and she is yours forever."

The robed and hooded man walked with the sure gait and demeanor of a seasoned warrior. Everyone who spied him walking into the drinking establishment could tell that. But when he walked up to the drinkmaster and brashly shoved a large ring of pure gold into his face, all thought him foolish. This was not the part of town to do such a thing, even if you are a seasoned warrior.

"Have you seen a ring of gold such as this?" the hooded warrior asked. This was his twelfth drinking house for the day and he had grown accustomed to the same answer. So when the drinkmaster reached under his table and pulled out an identical ring he was more than a little surprised.

"This is one just like it, right here," the drink master replied, showing it. "Good value, but it is just a gold ring. What is so special about it."

Lifting his own ring, the hooded warrior placed it right next the one in the hand of the drinkmaster. He turned his over, revealing the stamped sign of the Uas scepter, symbol of the royal treasury of Kemet. The drinkmaster turned his over, revealing the same symbol.

"Where did you get this ring?" demanded the hooded warrior, grabbing the drink master by the arm.

"Settle down, settle down," the drinkmaster said. "Let me think...ahh yes! It was the woman! The sad woman who used to come here a few weeks ago..."

"Do you know where she dwells?" the hooded man asked earnestly, "when did you last see her?"

Stepping back, the drinkmaster waved his hands palms up.

"We do not keep track of customer's whereabouts my friend, just their drinking preferences." he replied. "She liked strong drink, but they say she met the lotus dealer. Then she never came back."

"What lotus dealer?" the warrior replied from the shadows beneath the cloak. "Where can I find him?"

The drinkmaster shook his head.

"He disappears once in a while, returning with new stock. We don't know where he goes, but he left some men to peddle his loathsome wares while he is away."

"Where?" the hooded man asked, "Where are these men?"

"Did you see the three low lives standing across the street on your way in?"

The hooded man had checked the area well before entering the establishment. He did remember seeing three men across the street playing senet on a barrel.

"Those are the men?" the hooded warrior replied. "The senet players?"

"Oh they do more than play senet," replied the drinkmaster, "they take away my business with that foul lotus weed."

"Thank you atef," said the hooded warrior, turning around, "I will go and ask them."

As the hooded warrior was about to walk out the door, the drinkmaster called out to him:

"Atef, I would not do that if I were you. They are as bad as they come."

"No, they are not drinkmaster," the hooded warrior replied. "I am as bad as they come."

The three men standing around the barrel, an international collection of toughs gathered by their employer to tend to business in his absence, were also used to intimidate or worse when the need arose. The tallest was a sand dweller, who wore the traditional bushy beard of his kind and carried a long serrated dagger. He kept watch while two burley Kushite men played the game. So it was he who first saw the hooded warrior approaching and whistled, causing the two senet players to look up. They all had their hands on their daggers by the time the curious traveler stepped up to them.

"Greetings atefu," the hooded warrior said. "I seek information."

"If you don't seek lotus keep walking. And don't call us atefu, because we don't know you..."

"All men are atef, until they prove themselves different."

"Well we're different." grunted the tall sand dweller. "Buy some lotus or keep moving."

The hooded warrior stood for a second. Then he reached into a pouch at his waist and pulled forth a gold ring.

"If I purchase lotus will you give me some information then?"

"No!" growled the other Kushite, "Do we look like professional story sayers to you? Buy or push on!"

The hooded warrior placed the ring back. Then he sighed in resignation. He took off his cloak and hood, revealing a finely chiseled, muscular torso that looked as if it had been carved out of ebony wood. His hair was in long thick locks tied together, hanging down the middle of his back. A row of deadly darts, known to be the favored tools of a certain class of warrior feared for their battle prowess, was strapped around his chest. He carried two other weapons: a stick strapped across his back and sickle sword hanging at his waist. His people were known to hire themselves out to deal with men such as these, so the ebony warrior knew there would be no more discussion.

"Medjay!" cried the tall sand dweller, "gut him!"

His bronze hand went for his dagger, but was pinned to his thigh by a dart thrown with almost inhuman accuracy. As the man howled in pain the two Kushites charged forward with short swords drawn. Up went the ebony warrior's hand to snatch forth his fighting stick, as he lashed out with a swift kick to the nearest opponent's stomach. The man doubled over in pain as his friend slashed overhand, just missing the Medjay who swiveled aside with minimum effort, yet maximum skill. A loud crack rang out as his stick hit the doubled over warrior's head, causing him to crumble to the ground.

Meanwhile the sand dweller had extricated

the painful dart, only to be struck in the same wound by a fabled Medjay side kick. As he howled in pain once again, his remaining friend closed upon the Medjay, poking and jabbing with his short sword. The skilled ebony warrior parried the blade, ducked a wide slash, and then jumped back, seizing a dart from his chest belt.

"I grow tired of this," the Medjay declared. "Stand down! Now!"

Sensing movement behind him, the Medjay warrior fell flat. Then the dagger meant for his back sailed above him instead, lodging in the chest of his Kushite opponent. Rolling over, he saw the limping sand dweller approaching, short sword in hand. His long brown fingers were reaching for another dagger strapped to his leg, so the Medjay warrior threw his dart- right into the same wound he had stabbed and then kicked earlier. The sand dweller's eyes rolled back as he let forth a blood curdling cry. Then the tall bronze man fell over, his senses fading due to the intensity of the pain.

Surveying the scene, the Medjay took inventory: one man lay dead, killed by his own cohort's dagger to the chest, one man lay practically senseless with a dart sticking out of his quivering leg and the other was coming back around with a huge lump on his head. Concluding that lump head was his quickest source of information, the Medjay walked over and grabbed the dazed Kushite, yanking him to his feet. Lump head was made to look at the fate of his friends, and then the strong ebony arms pulled him nose to nose.

"I am Keshef, crown prince of the Medjay nation," the dangerous opponent declared, "and I quest to recover the love of my life. The next words emerging from your lips shall tell me how to find her, or those words shall be your last."

Chapter 8: The Strong Dominate the Weak

There was no sense of time in Nefertari's lotus induced nightmare. There were only cravings and satiation, along with feelings and images, day after day and night after night. She was aware enough to notice that Bekele had gone away, leaving her with a big Medjay warrior named Set-ja, who commanded many men and demanded that Nefertari lay with him in his tent in exchange for the lotus root. Nefertari did as she was told, enduring the strange man's sexual abuse time after time because Setja had what she needed: the golden lotus that was now Nefertari's life.

There were, of course, times when the lotus would wear off just enough to allow Nefertari some level of coherent thought. During these instances a slim chance would arise for her to manifest the will she had been taught during her spiritual lessons and warrior training. But accompanying these thoughts came the inevitable memories of her past life incarnation as mother of the Hyksos, which caused her true torture to come to mind: Nefertari's real addiction was to guilt.

When the lotus wore off the guilt inducing memories would arise, slamming against Nefertari's emotions like a tidal wave. A veritable avalanche of dead bodies – her valiant Theban relatives, babies sacrificed by the Hyksos and countless others would tumble across her mind, along with the taunting image of her dead sister urging her to go back to them. It was this that caused Nefertari's natural strength to fade, replaced by the conviction that she deserved to be enslaved by the lotus and to be the twisted object of the lusts of Setja. She reasoned, in her anguished guilt, that this was her atonement for the countless lives she had caused to be destroyed in her past lifetime. And so Nefertari decided, in her fleeting moments of clarity, that she was nothing more than a lowly nafis, that she'd keep chewing lotus to dull the pain, and accept whatever hardships came her way.

As the weeks wore on, Setja would often bring Nefertari into his main tent, displaying her as a sort of trophy to those who came to visit. At first he would send her away when he consulted with his men on important issues, but as time went by he would look over, note that his lotus addled consort was paying no attention and simply ignore her. But even in her weak minded state Nefertari noticed enough to realize that Setja was terrible man, a Medjay outcast with hatred in his heart and a plan for some sort of revenge.

Setja led his men, a strong force of bandits culled from the rejects of nearby nations, along the western oasis trail going north to the Great Green Sea. When they encountered strong forces along the way Setja would pretend to be a merchant, but when other caravans traveling along the trail appeared weak he would attack, plundering whatever riches they had, slaying many, and adding prisoners whom he would force march towards his ultimate destination.

At night in their tent, under the light of a candle, Setja would often unroll a papyrus map and study it. Poking at the parchment, his big finger would trail up a line that led to the shore of the northern sea, then resume in the green waters heading north. There the line snaked through a series of islands situated towards the middle of the green waters, where it finally arrived at its destination: a rocky piece of land marked by the head of the neter of chaos Set. It took seeing it many times for Nefertari's lotus crippled mind to grasp what she was looking at, but one night she realized where they were going. It was a place of legendary evil, a place that Nefertari had heard of all her life – a place that was feared by all who opposed the Asiatic invaders. Setja noticed the shocked look on Nefertari's normally placid face on that evening and confirmed it with a grim smile.

"Yes my sweet," Setja said, "after delivering slaves for many years, the Hyksos have finally given me permission to visit the great island. Set's Keep is our destination, and soon I shall have what I need to claim my rightful place as leader of the Medjay nation!"

After a trip that lasted a little more than two moons, Setja's caravan at last reached the shore of the Great Green Sea. It was a busy docking area, and large vessels were moored, rocking calmly on the waters of the ocean. But the calmness of the water was mocked by the bitter despair and tragedy displayed on the shore, as hundreds of captured, beaten and battered souls were lined up to be shipped off to slavery.

The captives, bound hand and foot, were of all sorts: Kushites of all varieties, including Kemites. bearded Shashu and their women from the eastern deserts, a few copper skinned outcasts of the Hyksos and many others. Even in her addled state, Nefertari could feel their grief and hopelessness as, walking side by side with Setja, they led his captives to join the doomed throngs.

10 of Setja's men led five wrist bound captives each via a rope tied from neck to neck. They walked down the docks towards the largest of the ships, where a hunch backed, bronze skinned man with a whip barked orders at everyone around him. Setja walked up to him and they greeted each other as friends. The man was clearly a Hyksos, and looked at Nefertari with obvious lust, causing Setja to grin and shake his head.

"This one is not for you Pa-uaum," he declared. "She is mine."

The hunchback stepped close and looked at Nefertari closely. He noted her barely open eyes and placid demeanor.

"Lotus is it?" Pa-uaum asked.

"Yes," Setja replied. "It keeps her...pliable."

"Ha!" shot back Pa-uaum, flexing the dangerous looking whip in his hand. "I much prefer the lash. Now lets see the rest of the stock."

Setja motioned towards his men and they brought the rest of the captives forward. Pa-uaum looked them all over, frowning at one exhausted, tattered Shashu woman with streaks of silver in her hair, then he came back over to Setja.

"They'll all do, except that one." Pa-uaum declared, pointing at the silver haired woman. "Too old."

Setja pointed at his men and they cut the woman loose and shoved her forward. Looking around in confusion, she wondered why she had been cut free.

"Feed her to the pigs," Pa-uaum declared.

Several men under the cruel whip master's control seized hold of the screaming woman and dragged her away. Both Pa-uaum and Setja watched without a hint of compassion. Nefertari looked on also, but she was chewing lotus, her blank eyes barely noticing what was occurring.

"Now then," Pa-uaum declared, "lets get the rest on board. We sail immediately for Set's paradise!"

The trip aboard the vessel took many days, and Nefertari began throwing up as soon as they got underway. Each day was more miserable for her than the last and she could keep no food down. At last Setja implored Pa-uaum to send in the ship's healer, who arrived in their cabin on the fourth day. She was an old Hyksos woman, with a hooked nose and a scowling, down turned mouth. After stomping into their quarters, she began poking and prodding at the sickly Nefertari, who was laying on a sheet atop some straw next to Setja's bed.

"I don't know why you have to bother me about a single slave," the woman grumbled. "I have to see to the entire ships cargo, and any who show signs of this much illness are simply thrown off. It saves me time."

Looking closely, the woman felt Nefertari's head, then her belly and finally shoved her hand between Nefertari' legs. She then nodded and turned to leave, hesitating briefly to spit out her findings.

"Put her on the bed and stop giving her lotus if you want them both to survive," the old Hyksos declared as she walked toward the door.

Setja's eyes widened.

"Both... What do you mean both?" he asked.

"She is pregnant fool," replied the healer over her shoulder as she stepped away. "About two moons and a half I suspect. I will send herbs to draw her off the root. Make sure she takes them if you want them to live."

Setja rushed over and carefully lifted Nefertari to his own bed. Then he slowly and firmly tried to pull the ever present lotus root from her hand. But she groaned and yanked it back, shoving it towards her mouth.

"That will be enough of that, little one," Setja declared as he forcefully tugged the lotus root away.

Nefertari responded with loud groaning and began thrashing around. But Setja, nearly twice her size, easily held her down. For long minutes Nefertari carried on, crying out for the lotus root until she finally drifted to sleep from exhaustion. Setja looked down at her finally serene face and smiled. Then he placed his hand upon her belly and stroked it tenderly.

"My son," the Medjay renegade said softly. "I know you are a boy. I know it. And after my enemies have fallen, you shall be prince of all the Medjay."

For the next five days Nefertari raged due

to being deprived of her precious lotus. Setja had to call upon the help of several men to tie her down to the bed and force the herbal drink from the healer down her throat. Many times the Meday outlaw grew tired and drew back to strike Nefertari into submission. But remembering she carried his child, he stayed his hand. Patience was not a virtue Setja drew upon with any regularity, but on this occasion, with a great deal of inner struggle, he called upon it.

Nefertari's outward struggle against the lotus proceeded, while her inner struggle with the mental assaults of her dead sister began again. As she drifted in and out of consciousness, her past life twin implored Nefertari to declare her identity to the people on Set's island when they arrived and come back to the Hyksos. Nefertari's sister shrieked out in her mind, taunting that she was already impregnated by a follower of Set and that the child tied her back to the Hyksos.

Nefertari's will power, eroded by bitter regret and moons of addiction to the lotus, was being slowly chipped away. To her great despair, Nefertari could feel her resolve slipping. But then, just as she was on the brink of giving in, her dead sister spoke no more. Upon closing her eyes, Nefetari could see her former sister's black eyed, ghostly form floating in her mind, but no words emerged from her moving lips. This brought Nefertari a measure of peace, enabling her to pay more attention to what was going on in the world outside her head. As she took notice it soon became apparent that the herbal potion being forced down her throat somehow silenced her tormenting sister.

So Nefertari started eagerly drinking it down, much to the surprise of Setja, and as the days wore on her spasms of withdrawal from the lotus subsided. Though the herb made her sluggish Nefertari could now think with a relatively clear head. But this meant that the feelings of guilt, intensified without the numbing effects of alcohol or lotus, hit Nefertari hard, making her hang her head low.

So when Setja confirmed the words of her dead sister, revealing that she was indeed pregnant with his child, Nefertari simply nodded, accepting it as part of her just punishment. Then later, in one of the fleeting times she would dwell upon her former life, prince Keshef came to mind. This caused Nefertari's emotional pain to double because, before the disastrous revelations about her past life, she had at last intended to accept his marriage proposal. But now, instead of marrying a Medjay prince, she carried the child of a Set following Medjay renegade - a fitting fate, she sorrowfully concluded, for the great betrayer of Kemet.

Nefertari thought back to when she first met the prince – of how brave and loyal he was in his pledge to protect her, even though she had ill treated him. Keshef had actually been smaller than her then, but that did not stop him from declaring his love and even protecting her with his life on that fateful trip to Djahy. Even after he grew into a mighty and handsome prince, with his choice of many others, his loyalty and affection for her had remained unwavering. But now, as sad tears were flowing from her eyes, her fervent wish was that the Medjay prince move on without her. Wanting the best for her beloved, Nefertari hoped that he would just forget about her, though she knew in her heart that she would never forget about Keshef.

Bekele was feeling satisfied. Aten beamed down upon his caravan as it made its way back north along Sebek's trail and he contemplated the success of his trip: He had several wagon's filled with his precious lotus, had negotiated deals back home for a better supply of the golden variety and he had placated the volatile bandit Setja with a great gift. The Kemit woman, Nefertari, that Bekele had given the bandit chief had crossed his mind several times on his journey, many more times than he thought it should. After all he had done such things many times before, having made the giving of women to powerful men a standard practice in his line of work. He considered it a cost of doing business. But why, Bekele wondered, did he have a strong feeling of foreboding about this particular woman? This feeling plagued the lotus dealer, even after they stopped at his favorite resting place along the route.

It was a well-watered island of lush trees amid the desert, a rather large oasis that usually set the mountain man's mind as ease. But the feeling about Nefertari did not flee even in his favorite surroundings, not even as he sat around a fire that evening watching his cook prepare meals. After supper was served Bekele sat back on his sleeping cushions, his belly full of the prized fowl he had brought back from his moun- tainous homeland. As he prepared to spend a rare night sleeping under the stars with his hired men, instead of in his covered wagon as usual, one of the guards hustled over and whispered in his ear. Looking up confused at first, Bekele looked over at the stranger standing on the edge of his camp. He then nodded, signaling to the guards to let the man approach.

The Kushite man walking toward the fire was surely a warrior, as his measured gait and strong demeanor denoted, but his long cloak and hood concealed his identity. As the man came close and stepped into the firelight he reached into his cloak, which made several of Bekele's guards pull weapons. Bekele himself leaned back ner- vously, though he was surrounded by several armed men. But the man merely yanked forth a small pouch, which by the sound of it was filled with some sort of metal. Bekele then relaxed, along with his men; for this was a sound he knew and loved.

"I am Keshef," the man said, pulling back his hood to reveal classic Medjay locs that reached the nape of his neck and deep ebony skin. "I seek Nefertari, a woman of Kemet."

Suddenly Bekele knew why he had been feeling uneasy about the woman. Here it was standing in front of him in the form of this dangerous looking warrior. The man was clearly going to be a problem and Bekele's first instinct was to order his men to kill him. But he had no way of knowing who was with this Keshef - he could have a hundred men waiting out in the desert.

"This Kemit woman," Bekele asked, "why do you want her? She told me she had no family, so what is she to you?"

Keshef's brow furrowed as he shot Bekele a hard look.

"That need not concern you." he replied, tossing over the clinking bag. "Here is gold. Where is she?"

The bag sailed from Keshef's hand over to Bekele's. The mountain man hefted it and found it quite weighty. Too weighty, he concluded, for Nefertari to be just a commoner. If she was attached in some way to a noble house, Bekele reasoned, he could be in for real trouble, so he decided the best thing he could do was to lie. Tossing the bag back to Keshef, he proceeded to do just that.

"She left along the way," Bekele stated. "She rode with us for a while and left the caravan in my mountain homeland."

"Oh did she now?" replied Keshef. "Then why did two of your men tell me you sold her..."

"What men?" Bekele blurted out, "who told you this?"

"Why, the perimeter guards I left lying out there." Keshef replied as he jutted his thumb over his shoulder. "When I asked they told me all they had seen in regards to the Kemit woman, so I let them live. I knew you would likely lie to me Bekele, but if you tell me where she is now I shall let you live too."

"I am afraid you are mistaken and those men were lying." Bekele replied slyly. "I don't know where Nefertari is now, so it is time for you to leave. Guards, show him the way out of our camp."

Several men stepped toward Keshef brandishing weapons. The Medjay backed up, his hands hanging by his side, then he turned as the men surrounded him.

"You should have taken the gold Bekele!" Keshef growled back over his shoulder as they marched him away.

"I have 25 men here!" Bekele shouted back. "If you return I shall have you killed!"

Bekele set extra men on perimeter patrol and stationed several more near him before settling into his sleeping blankets. After a night of fitful slumber he awoke to the familiar sounds of the camp breaking, but then he was given a most disturbing report: Two of the eight men he had sent out as perimeter guards were found dead while the other six had gone missing. Bekele frowned angrily and then ran out to the middle of the camp. Holding up a shiny gold ring, he shouted out to his remaining 17 men.

"A Medjay crept upon us in the night and slew several of your fellows!" Bekele cried, hoisting the ring even higher. "But it ends now! Delay breaking camp and go forth to slay him. Ten of these rings to the man who brings me his head!"

The men immediately stopped rolling tents and pulling up stakes, seizing swords and spears instead. Twelve men split into groups of four, then took off in four directions. Bekele held back five of his most trusted men for protection, then sat upon the ground to angrily eat his breakfast. As he tore into the dried meat and fruit he usually enjoyed so much, the lotus dealer barely tasted it.

"They will find that Medjay dog by noon." Bekele grumbled.

"Then I can be off and about my business."

But by noon Bekele's warriors started trickling in, dragging their wounded with them. Bekele stood staring in awe as the men returned from what looked like a major attack. But arrows jutting from non-lethal wounds, curious leg injuries and rope burns indicated the attacks were not intended to kill. Each of the returning groups had missing men and all had the same story to tell.

"Traps!" cried the men. "The Medjay has set traps all around the oasis! Ropes snatched men up into the trees, spikes stabbed us in the feet and legs from covered holes, and arrows struck us from out of nowhere!"

Bekele stood up, shaking his fists in a rage.
"He is only one man!"

"He is like a ghost, Bekele!" cried one of the injured men with an arrow jutting from his shoulder. "None saw him, and when we approached the source of a sound, the traps would spring upon us. I'm not going back out there!"

"Neither am I!" another petrified man cried.

"I am paying you to do your jobs!" Bekele shouted. Then the lotus dealer counted his men, finding only nine before him, half of them wounded.

"Where are the rest of them?"

One of the warriors being held up between two others due to a sharp wooden spike protruding from his foot spoke up.

"The Medjay tossed a gold ring to all those who would leave. Some took the payment and fled. I would have done the same were it not for this foot..."

"Arrrrrghh!" Bekele cried in anguished rage. Pulling his dagger, the lotus seller rushed up to the wounded warrior and stabbed him to death. His five personal guards stepped forward to back him in case those who carried the man objected to the murder, but the two men holding the would be deserter simply let his body fall and stepped back.

"There!" Bekele cried pointing at the man's body. "That is what happens to deserters! Pull stakes on this camp and stay in close formation. The Medjay dog can't come in and kill all of us!"

Bekele's wagon creaked forward as he cowered inside along with four of his warriors. The Amhari tried to feign courage, but he could not hold back the cold fear creeping into his heart. It seemed that the Medjay stalking them was a prime example of those cunning warriors of legend and he was beginning to regret ever meeting Nefertari. Bekele knew in his heart that this deadly Medjay loved her and very likely would not stop.

Meanwhile, as Bekele quaked in fear sitting atop his wagon in its covered section, Keshef hung silently in a sling tied to the bottom of it. As Bekele had distracted his men with his act of cowardly murder, the wily Medjay prince had crept into the camp, crawled under the wagon and slung himself securely to the undercarriage. It had been easy and would have even been fun if not for the dire nature of the circumstances. Keshef had gone out of his way to scare the Amhari's men so that he would have to kill as few as possible, but time was running out. A cold trail, as an old Medjay saying went, most often led to a cold body. So no matter how bloody the conflict turned, the prince grimly decided, it had to be ended soon.

As they made their way north along the route of Sebek's Way the Amhari's men looked all around them nervously. The landscape was bleak and sandy to the left, while the waters of the Red Sea lapped at the shore to the right.

One could see for miles across the desert in any direction, but still the men were on edge. Each looked around as if they expected the terrible Medjay to pop up from a sand dune and wreck havoc among them. Noting this, Bekele snarled, cursed and threatened, but his authority was no match for the fear instilled by the shadowy Medjay warror. Later that night the Amhari deployed his remaining men in a circular formation around their camp. Then Bekele at last settled in his own wagon, underneath his sleeping sheets, for what he thought would be a restful nights sleep.

But as soon as the Amhari started snoring hell broke loose.

Pulled from his slumber by loud panicked shouting, Bekele jumped down from his wagon with sword in hand. Before him was a huge fire -no, two huge fires- and as he squinted at the violent flames it dawned upon him: It was his two wagons filled with lotus root set aflame!

Instantly he began barking at his men, ordering them to fight the flames and save his product, but none answered. Looking around, he saw several dead bodies, each protruding with two or three of the deadly darts known as the primary weapon of the dreaded Medjay warriors. Bekele cursed this wretched arsonist, along with the entire Medjay nation, then shouted out in an attempt to rally the remaining men.

But they all ran away. Even the limping wounded were being helped along by others as, wild eyed with terror, they scampered off into the desert night. Bekele helplessly watched them go, then looked up at the blazing ruin of his lotus trade. He was finished and he knew it, his entire stock going up in smoke and there was no way he could replace it. Tears dripped from the Amhari's eyes as he first dropped his sword, then he dropped down to his knees, sobbing before the two soaring fires. For long moments he bowed his head and wept, and when he looked up there stood a muscular silhouette, framed dramatically by the light of the two flames, standing before him. Bekele felt the tip of a blade placed underneath his chin and his tear soaked face was tilted up. Then the Amhari locked gazes with two piercing, grayish brown eyes that seemed to peer right into his heart.

"Now then," the powerful dark figure surrounded by roaring smoke and crackling flames said calmly. "Where is my Nefertari?"

The island that the hunchbacked Pa-uaum called Sets paradise was just the opposite, which Nefertari noted as soon as they disembarked. Wretched slaves were being loaded and unloaded from vessels all over the busy docks, their cries and moans punctuated by the sharp crack of many whips. Flags and banners were everywhere, bearing the image and symbols of the neter of chaos. Besides the curious, long eared illustration of Set himself, many banners bore the image of his chosen animals: the pig, the hippo and the Apep serpent. Setja saw the disdain on Nefertari's face and chuckled as they walked along.

"The strong dominate the weak my dear," he declared. "This is how empires are run. Just be glad you are with me and not one of them."

As they passed a wild eyed Hyksos overseer beating a slave near to death, Nefertari was indeed glad she was not one of them. But this stood against everything she and her royal family had fought for and it was hard to hold her tongue about it. Nefertari had to remind herself again and again that she was no longer a princess, that it was no longer her job to protect people and that coming to this hellish place was all a part of her just punishment.

Setja turned in his captives and received payment, then she and the renegade Medjay were led to their accommodations: a little house a short distance away from the busy port. As they were escorted inside Nefertari heard curious squeaking coming from an odd looking, horse-shoe shaped dock a short distance away. Men were walking along it, some were leaning over, stabbing long spears into the bodies of some poor creatures in the water and then dragging them out with hooks. Nefertari heard a terrifying cry as one of the creatures was speared, then averted her eyes. Like so many other horrors on the island, Nefertari chose to ignore what ever the men were doing.

The little house was sparse, with a single bed, a cooking hearth and cupboard filled with dried meat and various fruits. Nefertari prepared a meal and they ate. Then both lay back upon the bed. It had been a long day, after a long journey and both she and Setja were tired. First Nefertari wanted to wash, but noted that a wa-tershed was not located in the rear area as they normally were in the houses of Kemet. She did find some soap though, and held it up curiously in front of Setja.

"You must come from a house of luxuries Nefertari." Setja chuckled as he pointed out a window toward the nearby sandy shore. "Take that soap and use the sea,"

Looking out the window, Neferari noted that the area was fairly isolated, then she stepped out the rear door and headed for the water. Stripping bare, she walked into water and be-gan to soap down. The waters were warm and soothing, and soon Nefertari began humming a song. After thoroughly washing, she lay atop the waves, floating in serenity. Just then Nefer-tari had the feeling she was being watched and looked out across the water to see a fin waver-ing and a large tail wagging back and forth. At first panic almost overcame her, but the creature blew water from a hole in it's head and Nefertari recognized it was not a shark. It was a dolphin, a water creature honored by the people of Kemet. Called the sea brethren by Kemetian tradition, the playful animals were protected from harm wherever they were encountered by her people. This dolphin slowly approached Nefertari and rolled over, flapping its flipper to splash her. Nefertari smiled and splashed back at it, then dove down into the water to join it beneath the waves.

As she approached the creature it lowered its bottle like snout, revealing a curious white patch upon its gray head. Nefertari rubbed the patch and the dolphin emitted soothing chirps and squeaks. As soon as the sounds were emitted, Nefertari felt waves of soothing emotions wash over her. The first feelings of true peace she had felt since that fateful day she learned of her past life. Along with the good feelings, memories of happy times in her childhood surfaced: sitting on her mother's lap enjoying her singing, playing with her twin Ahmesh and pranks played on members of her family and help staff. There were even memories of her father, who often hugged her with great affection before he too was lost early in her life in the wars with the Hyksos. Nefertari noted that the for the first time since the revelation, she could think about her past without the despair.

Nefertari drew closer to the dolphin, gripping its strong back fin, and it took off in a gentle dive. She held her breath as the animal flicked its tail, coming back to the surface just in time for her to catch her breath again, before diving back down again. The creature did this several times, to the great joy of the brown skinned, naked woman holding onto him. When the dolphin finally rolled away, Nefertari felt tears of joy rolling down her cheeks. Somehow this creature was helping to heal her, to get her to dwell on happier times and peaceful emotions!

The creature then started emitting different, urgent cries as it swam close to her, then swam away again several times. After several moments of this, it dawned on Nefertari that the creature wanted her to follow it somewhere. Just as she was about to swim after it, a familiar, harsh voice cried out.

"Nefertari!

She turned back to shore, spotted Setja standing there and started swimming back. Hesitating, she swept around to say farewell to her dolphin playmate, but it had disappeared. Nefertari then swam to shore and got out of the water, to find a scowling Setja peering down a her.

"You should not play with those animals." he said sternly.

"Why not?" Nefertari replied.

"Because they are livestock, that is why." he replied.

Nefertari was horrified and the expression on her face showed it as they walked back to the house. She said nothing, but as they slept later Nefertari dreamed of good things from her life as a princess for the first time since her past life revelation. She dreamed of life as a princess again. She dreamed of her family and of Keshef. But most of all she dreamed of dolphins.

Chapter 9: Why Won't You Bring Back My Child?

Nefertari remained in or near the small house they had been assigned, her belly ever growing as the weeks, then the moons went by. The accommodations were sparse, but the secluded beach upon which it sat was beautiful and Setja was gone during most of each day. For what purpose he'd leave he would not relay, but Nefertari was glad to be alone and away from the outlaw Medjay warlord, whose cold demeanor diminished only when he would dote over her swollen belly and brag of what a great warrior his son would be. She was told not to explore and obeyed accordingly, with the exception of swimming with her dolphin friend each day after Setja left. It was on such a day, late in her pregnancy during a twilight swim, that Nefertari's growing child and her dolphin friend turned her life around.

For the first few moons the dolphin had tried time and again to coax her to follow it. But Nefertari never did, afraid of where it would take her and concerned for its safety in case someone saw her with it. But she noticed that as the child inside her grew, it would kick and move gently in the presence of the dolphin. This strange reaction had become a source of joy for Nefertari - a joy she made sure to keep between herself, the dolphin and the unborn child.

On this particular day though, both the dolphin and the child were insistent. After a few moons of not trying, the dolphin swam back and forth relentlessly, keen on getting Nefertari to follow. But this time it seemed to have help, because the child in her belly would kick and strain against her womb in concert with the dolphin's movement. Finally Nefertari relented and swam after the dolphin, which made the child inside her finally calm down.

They left the area where they usually cavort-
ed, gliding past a sandy bend and out towards
an active shipping lane. Nefertari began to get
tired and tried to turn around, which made the
baby kick and kick. Suddenly the dolphin was
close, offering her a large back fin to hold on to.
Nefertari did just that, and felt the tremendous
strength of the creature as it flicked it mighty tail
and they took off.

After a few minutes the dolphin dove several
feet beneath the surface. It came back up only
to let the woman holding on get a good breath of
air, only to dive back down again. It quickly became apparent that her dolphin friend was being
stealthy and Nefertrari drew in close to help it.
Soon they came to an area teeming with wooden
cages that were built flush against a pier. The
wooden bars were thick and sturdy, built from
the floor of the sea to the surface. Inside these
cages writhed dozens of captive dolphins.

There were several men walking on the long
pier that ran parallel to the cages. One man
threw rotting fish parts into the cages, which the
apparently starving dolphins grabbed and ate,
but with little enthusiasm. Three other men approached one of the cages with evil sneers and
apparently wicked intentions. One carried a spear
and the two others had long poles with looped
ropes attached. The man with the spear leaned
forward and jabbed into the water, stabbing
into a dolphin which emitted a horrible mournful sound. As it was thrashing about, the two
other men dipped the ends of their poles in the
water until one of them looped the rope around
the screaming creature's tail. The powerful creature nearly pulled the man into the water, but his
companion braced him, and then looped his own
rope around the tail also.

Meanwhile, the man with the spear twisted it
in the dolphin's side, making it cry out in more
agony. Finally, after several minutes of thrash-

ing, the dolphin became limp and the two men dragged it out by its tail. It was still alive though, which caused the man with the spear to plunge the blade deep into its head, killing it. As the dolphin died it emitted a loud, keening, high pitched squeal, which was mimicked by the hundreds of other dolphins. It was the singularly most sad, mournful and pain wracked sound Nefertari had ever heard and brought tears to her eyes. All the dolphins, including the one she clutched onto, kept up the mournful death cry as the men dragged their brethren away.

Nefertari felt her child moving inside her, but in a different way than it had ever moved before. It was a soft, rocking back and forth movement and as the tears dripped down from her own eyes, she sensed her child was mourning for the tortured creatures also. A sad, silent moment went by as she floated with her dolphin friend, then Nefertari realized: This was the first time since her past life revelations she had shed a tear, had shown any concern at all, for any living thing besides herself.

And she began to feel ashamed.

Here was suffering right before her eyes in the form of these poor dolphins. But in truth she had been turning a blind eye to the suffering of others ever since she gave up her life as a princess. She had walked right past people in despair, enslaved, tortured and even killed, and had said nothing. She had spent all her time on this vile island ruled by Set cavorting in the ocean instead of trying to find out information that could burn the place to the ground.

Yes, Nefertari felt ashamed. But she determined right then and there that this would change.

Somehow the dolphin sensed her new resolve and as the moon rose it coasted near the cages to give Nefertari a good look at the entire complex. After an hour or so, several men left the pier, leaving two alone, obviously to guard

Princess Nefertari

the place overnight. Nefertari let go of the dolphin as the other men left and swam towards the pier. Looking up carefully as she tread water, she noted the two men were sitting near a flaming torch, bent over a game of Senet. Nearby their two spears lay propped against a pole.

Nefertari swam up to the pier and tried to pull herself up via a rope dangling on the side, but her swollen belly would not let her. Thinking for a moment, she decided on a different tactic.

"Help me! Nefertari cried, splashing about, "help me, I'm drowning!"

The two men jumped back from the board game and ran over to the side of the pier. There they saw a woman apparently struggling to get out.

"Here now," one man cried, "where did you come from?"

Nefertari leaned back, pretending to swoon and letting them see her swollen belly.

"Let us worry about that later, man. Can't you see the woman is with child?"

Both men leaned down and grabbed an arm, hoisting Nefertari upon the pier backward.

"Thank you, good atefs," Nefertari exclaimed, curling up to hide her privates. "It seems I fell in and lost all my cloths..."

Both men looked at each other, one displaying lust and the other concern.

"Don't even think about it!" warned the concerned one.

"Why not? She's here all alone..."

"Why she is at that..." the formally concerned man returned with a cocked eyebrow.

As the two men were debating the merits of raping her, Nefertari snatched up a spear, spinning it around to the wooden side. Both men looked at her, a naked woman with a swollen belly brandishing a spear butt, and broke out laughing. They did not laugh long before hard wood cracked across one man's skull, dropping him to the deck like a sack of wheat. The other man dodged Nefertari's straight thrust, only to be doubled over by a kick to the groin and felled by a sharp overhead strike to his temple.

As Nefertari snatched a dagger from the waistband of one of the fallen guards, she peered over into the cages. All the dolphins were now looking up at her, their heads rising eagerly just above the water. A quick glance out in the distance and Nefertari saw the white spot on her friend's head, also raising from the water as it looked on.

Bending down, Nefertari saw that each cage had a drop down door held in place by looped ropes tied into knots. There looked to be about twenty cages, so she went to work cutting the ropes and raising each one. Each time a cage door opened and the dolphins inside rushed out, they all let out a keening cry of exaltation and happiness. It took a few minutes, but finally Nefertari freed all the dolphins, tossed the knife next to the fallen guards and dove in herself.

Immediately she was greeted by her friend with the white patch, then many happy dolphins pressed in around her, keening with happiness. Nefertari got on the back of an especially large one and her white patched friend led them back to her cove. As she rode along she saw a small young dolphin swimming close by and noted a patch on its head almost identical to the one on the head her friend. Finally they came to the mouth of the cove and Nefertari slid off the big dolphin's back. Then they all gathered around Nefertari. Forming a huge circle, they arranged themselves like the petals of a flower. Extending outward nose to tail, their big blinking eyes beamed gratitude towards their liberator. Then suddenly they all began leaping high into the air, in a wondrous, joyful and acrobatic display under the light of the moon. For long moments Nefertari's breath was taken away by their graceful aerial show, then the crowd started dispersing and swimming away. They all went back to their watery homes, leaving only her dolphin friend and the little dolphin with the similar white patch to linger.

The big dolphin came in gently as Nefertari floated before it, rubbing its head against her swollen belly. Nefertari felt small kicks from her unborn child as it did this. Then the little dolphin came in and did the same thing. This time the child in her belly kicked and rocked gleefully and it dawned upon Nefertari: her patch headed friend was a mother! And, sensing Nefertari was too, it had lingered near her long enough for her baby to grow and through motherhood had established communication. The dolphin had reached out to her and in the course of Nefertari saving its child and the others, they had saved her from her long journey into despair and self pity! Nefertari hugged both dolphins, then the happy creatures took off for the open sea. Both jumped high into the air, where they were framed momentarily by the light of the full moon, before plunging down beneath the waves. As the dolphins disappeared Nefertari left the beach feeling lighter and peaceful. She went back to their little house to find that Setja was still gone, then retired to a truly restful sleep. Nefertari dreamed about her new finned friends and slept more soundly than any night she could remember.

But Nefertari's peace was not to last. Two days later Setja came stomping in as Nefertari prepared dinner. He was as sour as usual, but this time looked especially angry. Setja dragged a little girl in with him, shoved her into a corner and walked over to loom over Nefertari angrily. Slapping the wooden spoon Nefertari cooked with from her hand, Setja screamed at her.

"You!" he cried, stabbing his finger in Nefertari's face.

"What?" Nefertari cried. "What is it?"

"I had to kill two men today, and it was all because of you!"

Nefertari took a step back. At first she was confused, then she realized what he was talking about.

"The dolphins..." she whispered.

"They described the person who knocked them out and set those creatures free: a Kushite woman, heavy with child. It was you!"

Nefertari tried to back away, but Setja seized her by the throat with one big hand. Lifting her up on her toes, he reared back to slap her. Then he looked down at her swollen belly and carefully put her down.

"It took some doing, but I got it hushed up." Setja snarled. "I had to clean things up personally and then agree to do courier work!"

Then Setja pointed to the little girl. She was olive skinned with shoulder length black hair, big tear filled gray eyes and stood shaking with fear.

"Lowly courier work which is beneath me!" Setja howled, shaking his fist in the air.

Nefertari stood looking at the girl. Both had fear in their eyes as the huge man between them continued to rage. Seizing the child by her tiny arm, Setja flung her into Nefertari, who barely had time to brace herself to catch the girl.

"Until we get to Avaris she will be your responsibility." Setja ordered. "You will feed and cloth her, until the time comes when she is to meet her fate."

Nefertari looked down at the child, who could have been no more than seven years old, with utter horror as she realized what Setja was speaking about. Looking back up, she shook her head at Setja, but he simply laughed dismissively

"She is a child of Hyksos enemies." Setja sneered. "Her fate is sealed and there is nothing you can do about it. Her people should have made better decisions."

As Nefertari stood there hugging the child

in horror, Setja chuckled, picked up the wooden spoon and began shoveling food into a bowl. He took the bowl over to the table and as he sat down he growled out:

Oh, and tomorrow we sail back to the port and from there make our way to Avaris. Make sure the child is ready and make sure she behaves - or I will."

As he sat there eating, Nefertari took the little girl over to the bed. She tried to communicate with the girl, who mumbled a few undecipherable words in a strange tongue. There was obviously a language barrier, so Nefertari ceased trying and made the child lie down. Placing the girl's head in her lap, Nefertari hummed Kemetic childrens' songs until she drifted to sleep. As she stroked the child's hair with one hand, Nefertari looked over at Setja angrily, concealing the defiant fist she made with the other hand. He was a bad man, she knew. That he would kill in cold blood she had come to expect. But how Setja could so callously deliver an innocent child to be sacrificed on the bloody alters of Set, Nefertari could not understand. Nefertari was sure about one thing though, as she looked down at the innocent little face upon her lap: She was not going to allow that to happen.

Keshef glared through the window of the drinking house with his one exposed eye as he had done so many times before. There he saw the ships coming and going as usual, as well as those disembarking from them. This drinking house, and this particular window in it, was the best vantage point he could find for his clandestine purpose. Glancing around at the other spirit swilling patrons, he had to be sure he was not being closely watched. Those not tossing back beer were watching a knife throwing contest against a far wall. So Keshef reached up and scratched the ever present itch under the false patch over his left eye. Though thoroughly uncomfortable, it was part of his disguise as a sword selling outlaw and renegade from the Medjay nation.

It had been nearly seven moons since he had been told by the lotus dealer Bekeli that his beloved Nefertari had been turned over to a Medjay outcast named Setja. It had taken time, but Keshef had finally tracked the warlord to this port, a vile and lawless place under the control of the Hyksos. In order to learn what he needed, Keshef had concocted a disguise and faked an identity in order to ingratiate himself to some of the unsavory characters who ran the port. He took employ as a bodyguard for hire, but only during the night, so that he could watch the docks during daytime. He awaited the arrival of a Hyksos slaver, a hunchback with a cruel reputation, who had sailed away with the Medjay outlaw and a shipment of poor souls to be enslaved. This outlaw, it was said, had a beautiful woman with him who seemed to be somehow entranced.

But it was not entrancement, Keshef remembered with bitter anger, but lotus addiction. And for his part in it Keshef had made the evil Bekeli chew ten stalks of his own vile product, then left him writhing in the desert heat atop the smoking ashes of his wagons. No one would be spared who had in any way harmed Nefertari, Keshef had vowed. That included this Medjay renegade, this Setja. Even though it was said he was under the protection of the Hyksos, Keshef was determined that this warlord would feel his wrath.

After downing his second beer, Keshef saw a ship easing in to port. Its flag, wafting high in the air, displayed the emblem of Set. This caused Keshef to pay more attention. The drink master came over and tried to refill his cup, but he covered it with his hand. Continuing to peer out as the ship docked, Keshef observed those who started to disembark. Soon he spotted the hunchback. As described the deformed man cracked a whip and shouted out in as unruly a fashion as possible. This was definitely the ship, but did it bring those he sought?

For a few more moments Keshef watched as those aboard disembarked. Then a small knot of people came down the gangplank – a large Kushite man surrounded by several tough looking warriors. And by the side of the big man there strode a Kushite woman, heavy with pregnancy, clutching the hand of what seemed to be a child from some northern land. As they got closer, Keshef gasped. Two shocks hit him like a cudgel: The woman with child was indeed Nefertari and the big man was someone he knew years ago as a child: it was his very own cousin!

Setja and his entourage saw a drinking house and swept inside with haste, eager to wash away the sea water from their throats. The drink master frowned at the pregnant woman and small girl who accompanied them, but ignored them after Setja tossed a small silver ring upon the counter. As Nefertari and the girl sat quietly in a corner, Setja looked around, scanning his surroundings as a true warrior always does.

Men were having a knife throwing contest nearby and most others were simply drinking. One man with a patch over one eye glanced their way, but quickly turned up his beer and looked elsewhere. It was a typical bar scene, Setja thought, though there was something interesting about the patch eyed drinker. After a couple of rounds, several of his men joined in the knife throwing contest, slapping silver rings down in wagers. Setja nodded proudly as his men eliminated the locals in the competition, then began wagering with each other.

Suddenly the patch eyed man stood up, tapped his table and cleared his throat. Everyone turned around. The patch eyed man tossed a silver ring toward the knife throwing group, which one of them caught and slapped down on the table. Then a dart sailed from the patch eyed man's hand, from twice the wagering distance away from the target and at an angle. The target was hit dead center. The patch eyed man walked over and snatched up all the silver rings upon the table, except one, which was covered by the hand of one of Setja's largest and meanest looking men.

"Who asked you to join us?" the big shashu tough growled.

"You did not toss the wagered ring back," patch eye replied, looking at the other men. "I threw and I won."

The other men nodded, gesturing for their friend to honor the wager and take his hand off the ring. But the big shashu merely ground his teeth and began inching his other hand toward his dagger. Patch eye stomped on his foot, causing him to bend over, howling in pain, then followed up with a knee to the forehead. The man fell over, out stone cold as the patch eyed man plucked up the silver ring.

His cohorts all pulled daggers and where about to leap in defense of their downed man, but a whistle from Setja halted them. The patch eyed man didn't flinch as he pocketed the silver ring and then nodded at Setja. The big man hoisted his beer in a salute while humming a Medjay song. Then he began reciting the Medjay initiation saying:

"A medjay..." Setja began.

"Is a lion!" finished the patch eyed man.

Then Setja and the patch eyed man recited simultaneously:

"We are not prey!"

Setja swept his fingers at his men and they dragged their unconscious comrade over to a table and propped him up on a chair. Then, locking eyes with his assailant, Setja swept his hand towards a seat at his table. The patch eyed man walked over and sat down.

"Thank you for not killing him," Setja said as he shoved a mug of beer across the table to him.

"He was rude. Who says I won't kill him when he wakes up?" replied the patch eyed man as he lifted the brew.

Setja smiled, took a long pull of his beer, then banged the mug on the table. Wiping his mouth with the back of his hand, he laughed heartily.

"Ha haa! I like you!" Setja proclaimed, pointing at patch eye. "Who are your people? The Dune Runners? Its the Runners correct?"

Not wanting to disappoint the big man and knowing enough about that particular section of the Medjay nation to fake it, the patch eyed man nodded affirmatively.

"I knew it! You scorpion eaters are as tough as they come!" Setja howled. "So what did you do to get banished?"

"I killed a man over a woman."

"Really? Was it a fair fight.?"

"There was no fight. I simply killed him." replied patch eye.

"And what of the woman?"

"Pushed her into the Blue Nile after I was done with her."

"A little murder, a little tossing women into rivers...that will do it." replied Setja with a grin. "So what are you doing for work?"

"A little of this and a little of that," replied patch eye, holding the mug in front of his mouth. "What are you into?"

"A lot of this and a lot of that." replied Setja slyly, eyebrow raised. "Come work for me. You get to keep all you take on raids except for a quarter that you pass back to me. Bonuses are plentiful for special jobs and you keep half on any slave you bring in for sale."

"Sounds fair," replied patch eye. Then he pointed at the unconscious man. "But won't he be angry you hired me?"

"Oh he'll get over it. If not you have my permission to kill him..."

Setja and the patch eyed man both chuckled, then clinked mugs and downed the rest of their beers.

Meanwhile at a table nearby, Nefertari was trying hard to keep her composure. Though he was wearing a disguise, she recognized the patch eyed man as her beloved Keshef. Tears nearly came to her eyes as she contemplated the depth of his love and loyalty, because she knew he had come to save her.

For the first few days on the road Nefertari was careful not to come anywhere near Keshef. As the caravan left the area near the Great Green Sea and began heading southwest toward Avaris, Setja and Keshef spent a great deal of time together, making the situation much more dangerous. Keshef played the game masterfully as they swapped Medjay tales, often referring to Nefertari as Setja's "serving girl" as she waited upon them. Never once did he catch her eye, nor she his, because the stakes were too high to be discovered. Nefertari had three lives to take into consideration, four including Keshef, and both realized that the timing of their move would have to be impeccable. It wasn't until over a week had passed, as they both bent to dip water from an oasis spring, that they found themselves alone and able to speak freely.

"Nefertari." Keshef said as he bent to fill his water flask. "The time is rapidly coming. Tomorrow night I am on perimeter watch. I'll subdue the guards just past the mid hour of night. Then we take a wagon and leave."

"I can't go without the girl." Nefertari replied. "Please let us take her also."

Keshef nodded.

"Aum Mat Ra told me what lies in store for her," he replied.

"Bring her, but move quickly and quietly."

Looking up with confusion, Nefertari replied: "Aum Mat Ra? Are you speaking of Setja?"

"Aum Mat Ra is his birth name. I know because he is my cousin..."

Nefertari nearly fell over into the water.

"Your cousin! I thought he was lying. He is always claiming royalty...."

"My uncle and his family were banished for dealings with the Hyksos," Keshef returned. "It is a long story for later. Can you make sure he is asleep?"

"I can," replied Nefertari. "We will be ready."

The next night Nefertari served Setja his favorite meal, Nile trout with heaps of spiced onions and potatoes. As he sat back patting his stomach, she poured him plenty of his favorite beverage, a strong wine from the orchards of the Hyksos, while questioning him relentlessly and annoyingly about his life as a Medjay warrior. By the time she was done plying him, Setja was stuffed full and mentally exhausted.

Lying next to a snoring Setja in their covered wagon, Nefertari pretended to sleep. Her eyes wide open, she looked down at his big hand caressing her swollen belly. This had been his nightly ritual since she became pregnant, and for all his flaws, she knew he truly cared about his child. Setja had long ago figured out Nefertari was not of peasant blood, and was glad he had created a child with a woman of quality. It was going to break his heart to discover that she was gone, along with his dreams of parenthood and lineage.

The hours ticked by. Nefertari leaned over from their sleeping blankets and pushed open the flap to the wagon. Up in the sky the moon was directly overhead, signaling that the time had come. Carefully Nefertari removed Setja's hand, then squirmed away from him. She did all she could to be stealthy, but as she got up, Setja growled groggily:

"Where are you going..."

Nefertari stood stock still. Then she came up with a ruse.

"The child had to relieve herself, and we don't want her doing it in here."

"Oh." Setja replied with a yawn. "You'd better take her out then..."

As Setja rolled over and began snoring, Nefertari crawled over to the little girl, lightly shaking her. The girl sat up and Nefertari pressed a finger to her lips. Pushing a bag full of water bottles and food she had gathered earlier into the girls arms, Nefertari turned to get a valuable prize she could not leave behind.

On the far side of the wagon there was a small chest. This was where Setja kept his most prized possessions, including the map to Set's Island. Nefertari crawled over stealthily and first grabbed a cloth bag she often used to carry food and other items. Then she slung it over her shoulder, scooted up to the chest and scooped it up. Placing it inside the bag, she signaled to the little girl to be quiet and they carefully pushed open the flap and slid down to the ground.

Looking around carefully, Nefertari found that the caravan was quiet and still. They had parked in a straight line up against a rocky hill. Looking both ways, Nefertari spotted a flaming torch waving near the front wagon. She took the girl's hand and headed for it. When they got there Keshef stood over two guards, both obviously dead. He had pulled out most of the contents of the front wagon and it lay strewn near the deceased guards.

"What of the perimeter patrol?" Nefertari

whispered as Keshef helped them into the wagon. "There are usually several men out there..."

"Now there are none," replied Keshef.

"But won't they hear the wagon, the horses as we get going?" Nefertari asked. "There are nearly fifty men here. We will wake up the entire camp when we get underway."

"Don't worry Nefertari," Keshef replied. "There was a reason I suggested to Setja that we camp here. I told him we needed our backs to a wall for security and he agreed. Of course I had to go up the hill to ensure it was safe from rock falls..."

"So how does this help us?" Nefertari shot back.

"This hill is not safe from rock falls," replied Keshef calmly. "and I helped a bit..."

Then the Medjay prince ran a third of the way of the hill, where he kicked a log. That log fell away, releasing another log placed on an angle above it, which let loose a large stone that rolled and hit other stones. A small rumbling began that got louder and louder as Keshef ran back down, jumped into the wagon and snapped the reins. The horses began trotting, pulling them off to a safe distance just as a large avalanche of boulders began raining down upon the camp. Several wagons were smashed to pieces, along with the men inside who howled in terror. Sounds of screaming and people running back and forth followed them as Keshef, Nefertari and their little charge bound away into the night.

Their escape afforded time for long needed conversation, so each relayed their stories through the night. Even their little charge was able to communicate that she was called Pudhukhpa. Near dawn all were exhausted from the escape and the discussions about their lives, so they found a high hill to park upon and slept well into morning. Nefertari did not know exactly how much time had gone by, but when she was shaken awake by Keshef Aten was quite high in the sky.

"Get up Nefertari," he said with concern. "It seems the trap did not slay him. My cousin is on our trail."

Nefertari squinted as she rose, then looked down the hill to where Keshef was pointing. In the distance she saw a wagon. There were several men on it and it was moving fast. What concerned Nefertari most was that they had four horses, which meant that they could catch up to them easily.

"Fear not," Keshef said. "I know a way to escape them. There is a bridge not far from here. It goes over a gorge..."

"Then let us get there," Nefertari replied.

They took off at a fast trot, frequently looking behind as those who pursued gained on them. After an hour or so, they could hear their pursuers, and could see Setja snapping the reins mercilessly. They got within shouting distance just as the gorge and bridge came into view. It was a simple bridge of wood, wide enough for one wagon and supported by sturdy ropes. Keshef urged their tired horses on and they crossed just as Setja got to it. Leaping down, Keshef pulled his dagger and began hacking away at the rope on one side. Nefertari scrambled over to the other side and began cutting rope loose. An arrow suddenly landed between them.

"I told you not to shoot at them!" shouted Setja at the man next to him holding a bow. With an angry growl, Setja pulled his dagger, plunged it into the man's chest, and kicked him over into the gorge. As he held his remaining two men back from trying to cross the bridge, Setja shouted:

"Nefertari! Please don't do this!"

There was real anguish in his voice, and somehow Nefertari found herself feeling sorry for him. But she simply rolled her eyes and kept cutting. At nearly the same time, she and Keshef chopped through the last of the rope and their end of the bridge fell away in to the chasm.

Setja screamed"

"Noooo!"

Then Keshef stepped forward, removing his eye patch.

"It is over Aum Mat Ra," he pronounced. "You shall never again be near this child."

Setja's jaw dropped. His face contorted as he looked afresh at the face of the man he had simply called "Patch."

"No one knows that name but my family!" he cried in utter astonishment. Then recognition finally began to settle in. "Keshef...is it you?"

"Yes it is I cousin," Keshef replied.

"But wait...I heard you were courting a princess of Kemet...."

Then Setja's jaw dropped even further.

"A princess named... Nefertari! But this means...this means my child is entirely of royal blood!"

Then Setja looked toward Nefertari.

"Why did you not tell me!"

"That was my old life," replied Nefertari. "And it was not for you to know."

Setja's face contorted in true despair. Then he backed up behind his men and kicked one of them into the gorge. As the man fell screaming, the warlord stabbed the other in the back and threw him over also. Then Setja dropped his weapon and got down on his knees.

"Look what you make me do! I had to slay my own men so that they would not see me begging. Cousin, you know how important lineage is to our people! Why won't you bring back my child?"

"You don't deserve to parent this child. You are a betrayer of the Medjay people." Keshef shot back.

Suddenly Setja dropped his head and began to sob. Moaning deeply he turned toward the mother of his unborn child.

"Nefertari...please Nefertari, let us work something out. Please don't take my baby from me..."

Nefertari shook her head, then she beckoned little Pudhukhpa to come forward. Placing one hand on the girl's shoulder, Nefertari pointed across the gorge accusingly.

"You would deliver the child of another parent to be cruelly sacrificed on the alters of Set, yet you beg to be the parent of the one I carry! You are an evil follower of an evil tradition Setja! You don't deserve to see this child be born. From this day forward the fruit of my womb is mine alone and you shall never, ever be near us again!"

With that, Nefertari, Keshef and Pudhukhpa got back into the wagon and started away. They did not look back, but they could hear Setja's bitter sobbing and his anguished, mournful cries echoing across the gorge:

"Noooo! Cousin! Bring my child back! Nefertari! Please bring our baby back to me!

Pleeeese! Pleeeese! Pleeeese!"

Chapter 10: The Means to Destroy Set's Island

The Red Sea Hills loomed up ahead as the parched, weary horses slowly dragged their wagon across the hot desert sands. Aten beamed down relentlessly, making the wagon's three thirsty riders intensely dry of mouth – so much so that it almost made Nefertari regret her decision not to return to Kemet. Almost, but not quite.

"Are you sure about this beloved?" Keshef asked for the hundredth time. "Your family needs to see you. Your people need to know that their beloved princess is still alive."

Nefertari shook her head.

"I told you I am not returning to Kemet," she replied. "I am...unworthy..."

Keshef opened his mouth to protest further and Nefertari put her hand over his lips.

"Please Keshef," she implored. "Lets just find the water you promised would be here on the road to your Medjay homeland."

Keshef sighed and again conceded defeat. Though they had argued about it many times during their journey, on this issue Nefertari would not budge. It had been ten days since they had escaped Setja and immediately Keshef had turned south towards Waset to take Nefertari home. But she had insisted otherwise, so they found themselves on the road to the capital city, indeed the only city, of the nomadic Medjay nation. Now they traveled southwest, across the dry hills and mountains adjacent the Red Sea, to a fabled oasis set in a valley called the Het (meaning home) of Apademak. It was a location purposely chosen by the Medjay people because the path to it was completely waterless, ensuring that only those who could read the secret signs could get there. As the wagon neared an especially steep, rocky hill, Keshef spotted one such sign.

It was a gigantic paw print that his people called the sign of Apademak, the just war neterwith a lion's head revered and emulated by the Medjay people. It was carved into the rock cliff face in such a way that an untrained eye would see only jagged lines, but to Keshef it pointed the way to a stash of water buried beneath it. Keshef stopped the wagon, jumped down and ran over to the cliff as Nefertari and Pudhukhpa watched eagerly.

Stepping up to the cliff face, he tapped his foot on the ground nearby a few times, then began digging in the sand with his bare hands. Pudhukhpa and Nefertari soon joined him and after several minutes they dug out a large vase sealed by a tightly tied, waxed cloth. Tearing the cloth off, they all plunged their hands inside, scooping out handfuls of water. After filling their bellies, they gave some to the horses and got back under way.

After a day or so they crested a huge red hill and looked down. There they saw a large valley, filled with thousands of tents, surrounding a wooden temple that sat before a large lake with sparkling blue water. Suddenly several warriors appeared, seemingly out of nowhere, emerging from behind rocks and shrubbery. They saluted Keshef, then beckoned them forward as they led on.

"Where did they come from?" asked Nefertari

"They have been watching us since shortly after we found the water," Keshef replied. "Welcome to my home Nefertari - Het Apademak!"

The Medjay sentries led their wagon towards the waterline of the great blue lake, then they followed the shoreline towards the great temple. As they went along word spread of their arrival and many people emerged from their tents to cheer for Keshef. It seems that his quest was common knowledge and they jumped for joy when they saw Nefertari. Many shouted out in their exuberance:

"Mighty Keshef has done it!"

"Prince Keshef found his princess!"

"All salute Princess Nefertari!"

Upon hearing the crowd call her princess Nefertari shook her head. Then she covered her face with a blanket and finally leaped from the driver's cab back to the covered section. She refused to come out no matter what the crowd or Keshef said. Crawling to the sleeping mat inside, Nefertari buried her face in a pillow and tried to block out the cheering by covering her ears. Little Pudhukhpa did her best to comfort her, finding their roles strangely reversed as she stroked the despairing Nefertari's head in her own lap.

At last they stopped before the temple, which, although made of wood, was huge and beautifully crafted. Nefertari peeked out from the wagon's cloth flaps to find they had stopped before a living example of the ancient sacral places she had seen on walls and in old scrolls. Huge logs that must have come from the forests of Behktan had been cut and formed into an edifice similar to the fabled temple of Ausar. The walls were smooth, painted purple and had been illustrated to look like the even earlier reed temples of the Kushite ancestors of the Medjay and Kemetic peoples. The beautiful walls were topped by a white flat rooftop covered in lion paws and full bodied illustrations of the Neteru Apademak in all his man bodied, lion headed glory. There were illustrations of Sekmet, ancient female Neteru of motherhood and protection also revered by the Kemetic people. This confused Nefertari and she pointed at the illustrations, looking to Keshef with raised eyebrows.

"Sekmet and Apademak are mates," Keshef said. "It is a very old tradition that we have never given up."

Several people emerged from the temple and

came towards them as they stepped down from the wagon. Nefertari recognized Prince Pakhu, though he had a smidgeon of gray in his long locs. A few others approached also, all wearing simple Medjay attire except the exquisitely crafted, wide necklaces that designated Medjay royalty. A very old woman held onto the prince's arm for stability as they approached. Behind them came a younger woman and several children.

Before they all could give their greetings, Keshef held up his hand to stop them. Leaving Nefertari near the wagon, Keshef took them aside and spoke to them in hushed tones. Nefertari saw the elder woman glance over towards her, shaking her head with annoyance. Finally Keshef beckoned to Nefertari and she walked over towards them.

"Hail and greetings Prince Pakhu," Nefertari said with a deep bow.

"Hail and greetings to you also Nefertari," the prince replied.

Then he gestured towards the elder woman. "Let me introduce you to Queen Mut Shem Sut." Nefertari bowed even deeper because she was addressing a very aged elder.

"Hail and greetings Queen Mut Shem Sut!"

"Hail and greetings to you also young woman, though I still can't understand why I can't call you what you are..."

Prince Pakhu frowned at her.

"Mut!" he cried.

"I am too old for pretension and for caring about hurt feelings," his Mut returned in an aged, crackling voice. "What ever happened to this girl has not changed her bloodline. If one of you ever came home spouting such nonsense..."

"Mut please!" Keshef cried. "She is with child and has had a trying time. Let us just deal with that."

The elder queen frowned, then looked down

Princess Nefertari

at Nefertari's swollen belly. She then nodded.

"So we should. Clean her up and then bring her to me. Now take me back in to prepare son..."

Prince Pakhu nodded at everyone, then led his Mut back into the temple. As they disappeared inside the younger woman shooed away two young boys and a smaller girl, then approached Nefertari.

"I am Princess Nit, wife of Prince Pakhu," she said. "Our little ones you can meet later. Come, let us get you rested and prepared for Queen Mut's examination."

Keshef left to attend to other business and Nefertari followed Princess Nit inside the temple. They walked through several large rooms, all decorated with the illustrations of Apademak, Sekmet and several other Neteru that Nefertari had never seen before. At last they came to a large room that was a built around a small inlet of the lake. Neferari was led up to it and found that part of the temple wall formed an arch over a small finger of the lake, letting its cool waters flow inside the room for swimming and bathing. Several servant girls were there with soap and oils and they disrobed Nefertari and led her into the cool water. The servant girls scrubbed her down from head to toe, dried her off with soft towels, then put a robe on her.

Princess Nit sat waiting until the job was done, then led Nefertari to another chamber. This one was dominated by the illustrations of Sekmet and Bes, the little dwarf Neter known for watching over children and blessing childbirth. Princess Nit led Nefertari towards a long table and handed her two small mugs. One was filled with water and the other was empty.

"Drink," ordered Princess Nit. "The other cup is for when it comes out. We keep it to show the Queen Mut."

Nefertari nodded and drank the water. They made small talk for a while, then Nefertari squatted and filled up the other cup. She then handed the yellow liquid to Princess Nit, who took it and placed it on a nearby small table. The princess then exited, saying over her shoulder:

"I'll get the Queen Mut now."

Several minutes later Princess Nit led the elder Queen Mut back into the room.

"Where is the pee?" the elder queen demanded.

Princess Nit led the queen over to the table. The elder woman picked up the cup, looked at it, then sniffed it. She frowned and then gestured for Nefertari to lie down. Pulling open the robe, the elder queen put her ear to Nefertari's belly, then poked and prodded her breasts and between her legs. She pointed at a small vase on a table across the room and Princess Nit brought it to her.

There was a waxed cloth covering the vase which the elder twisted off. Reaching inside, she pulled out a pinch of yellow powder. The queen popped the powder inside the pee cup, picked it up and then swished it around. She took another pinch of the powder and approached Nefertari on the table. As she got closer, it became apparent what the elder intended to do and Nefertari closed her legs. The queen frowned at her, clicked her tongue impatiently and asked:

"Do you care about the infant?

Nefertari nodded affirmatively.

"Then open your legs and stop acting like a child..."

Nefertari complied and the queen shoved a finger coated with the yellow powder inside her. There was slight pain, which made Nefertari writhe, then it was gone, replaced by a slight tingling. The elder queen pulled her finger out, looked at it and shook her head sadly.

"What have you been doing to yourself young lady?"

"What are you talking about? Nefertari replied.

"You know what I am speaking of." the queen

retorted. "Don't play games with me. What have you been putting inside your body."

Nefertari thought for a moment. Then she lowered her head in shame.

"It...it was lotus."

"I thought as much," the elder said. "You have done too much damage Nefertari. The child will not survive birth."

Nefertari gasped in absolute shock. Then Princess Nit was there, holding her hand and looking down sympathetically.

"Queen Mut," the princess said. "Are you sure?"

"The lotus has poisoned her womb," Queen Mut Shem Sut replied sadly. "Nothing can come forth from there alive."

Nefertari looked down at her belly and began to sob. Tears began to streak Princess Nit's face also.

"But..." said Princess Nit hesitantly, "but what about the power place."

The elder queen looked down at Nefertari sadly. Sighing, she locked eyes with Princess Nit and shook her head.

"It is too far gone. The damage too extensive. Even if we take her to the place of power for healing only one of them could survive. I am sorry..."

Nefertari reached out and seized the elder's hand. Looking up through her tears, she whispered intensely:

"If there is a chance to save my child, please let me take it."

The queen looked down at her with pity.

"The choice Princess Nit speaks of could only save one of you Nefertari. The best thing is for you to give up on this baby and go on to live your life. You have people who care for you, especially Keshef..."

"I have no life!!!" Nefertari blurted out tearfully.

Both the queen and Princess Nit looked down at Nefertari's tear soaked face as her whole story came tumbling out. She told them all about her past life revelation as the progenitor of the Hyksos, her utter despair about it, her mental torture at the hands of her dead sister, her time enslaved to the lotus and her time with Setja. Nefertari felt only shame, but the two royal women felt pride that she had endured such tragedies and lived to tell. They came to understand Nefertari and so were prepared when she declared:

"I cannot stand the thought of causing the death of another child, especially my own! Please bring me to this place of power! Please help me save my baby!"

Queen Mut Shem Sut looked down at Nefertari for a long moment, then declared:

"So be it."

Nefertari lay paralyzed, encased inside a mound of earth high atop a nearby mountain, in a spot renowned for being saturated with the primordial power of Geb. A trench had been dug beneath her so that she could relieve herself and a hole had been left for her to breath through and be given sustenance. But her eyes were covered, no part of her body was exposed and she was sealed like a mummy in a tomb. Only a few Medjay women, led by Queen Mut Shem Sut and Princess Nit had been allowed on this sacred peak. It was they who carried sacred, blessed water up the mountain, kneaded the earth into mud, and had encased it around Nefertari. She remembered her final sad words to her beloved Keshef as she embraced him at the foot of the mountain:

"The child is of your blood Keshef. Queen Mut says it is a boy. If I manage to save him, please take care of him the best you can. And don't forget you will forever be my beloved."

Keshef stood and watched as they disappeared up the mountain, and it was this image of him that had kept Nefertari strong for the nearly two weeks she had been entombed. She had been given the proper breathing instructions and could feel the power of Geb seeping up from this sacred peak and swarming towards her womb. Her baby would kick as she concentrated on pre-serving it's life, but she could feel her own limbs getting weaker and weaker. Nefertari sensed she would not survive long after the birth due to the healing energy going to the child and not to her-self. But she had accepted this, so when labor started she was glad that it would soon be over and hoped her child would be safe.

As her contractions got closer and closer, she began to get delirious. Many images flashed through her mind and she began to hear mem-bers of her family. She especially heard her Mut, Queen Ah Hetep, and imagined that she was there watching over her. Little did Nefertari re-alize that her Mut was actually there, having been fetched by Keshef from Kemet. Queen Ah Hetep and her brother Ahmesh had been there for nearly a day, and were determined to find a way to save Nefertari or be with her as her spirit passed on. As Nefertari's contractions intensi-fied, the Medjay women dug the earth away from her, while the two queens conferred about an idea tabled by Nefertari's Mut.

"Do you think this will actually work Ah Het-ep?" asked the elder queen.

"My daughter has no other options, so it must work," the queen of Kemet replied. "We have much experience with placenta magic in Kemet, but we shall require your help and the assistance of the sire of the child or a close male relative."

"Well the child's sire could never come here," replied Queen Shem Sut, "but we do have one of his blood."

Queen Mut Shem Sut summoned Keshef, who stood apart speaking to Ahmesh outside the ring drawn around the birthing area. Men were forbid-den to step into it, but the queen gave Keshef special permission. The two queens then told him of their plan to save Nefertari, but Keshef needed more clarity so it had to be explained to him.

"The placenta, Keshef, is the protective shield for a child in the womb," explained Queen Ah Hetep. "It sends food, air, water and filters the womb for the betterment of the child. Like the child itself, it is formed from the unity of the man and woman and is birthed along with the baby."

"It also acts as a director and accumulator of the healing powers that come from the sire's blood," continued Queen Shem Sut. "These healing powers are a gift from the male, acting as an internal defense and strengthener of the womb, just as the man is the external defender of family in society."

"The healing that Nefertari has given to her child must flow through the placenta and it is our hope that it has accumulated enough healing force to be given back to her," said Queen Ah Hetep. "But we need your help because only the blood that helped create the placenta can intensify and facilitate this healing. And in a situation this dire, it must be directed by the will of a true warrior."

Keshef nodded.

"I see, and since the real sire is not here, you hope that I as a close relative can direct this healing force?"

"So we hope. And your feelings for Nefertari will help," replied Queen Shem Sut. "But it is dangerous. If you give too much of yourself... you could die..."

Keshef shook his head.

"I do not care. I will do it."

Both queens smiled at Keshef, then directed him to lay down next to Nefertari. As Aten went down and the moon rose, they encased Keshef inside the sacred mud while Nefertari was finally uncovered and washed down to give birth. Keshef did as he was directed, and for hours concentrated on the image of Nefertari as a healthy young woman. Keshef could indeed feel the power of Geb in this sacred place. It flowed into him, washed over him and writhed around him like a giant snake. It was intoxicating, it was distracting, and he understood why they needed the will of a warrior. Without his mental training for combat and Ra force direction, he would be at the mercy of the power, instead of seizing, directing it and mastering it for the sake of his beloved.

Meanwhile, Nefertari's womb finally opened and the Medjay women pulled forth a howling boy child. Quickly they handed the baby over to Queen Ah Hetep, who held her precious grandchild as they awaited the birth of the placenta. It emerged minutes later and was immediately buried between Keshef and Nefertari. As they quickly piled earth back on top of her, the now fading Nefertari's breathing became more ragged and shallow. Hearing this Keshef focused even harder on the rhythmic breathing he had been instructed to do, all the while concentrating on healing his beloved.

Queen Mut Shem Sut gathered the Medjay women into a circle, then they held hands and began an ancient Kushite healing chant and Het Heru healing dance. They chanted louder and louder, all the while directing their energetic hymns and sensuous, womb enhancing movements at Keshef and Nefertari. Queen Mut Ah Hetep handed her grandchild to a nearby woman. Stepping forward, she too began the Het Heru healing movements between the entombed couple. Waving her hands over the buried placenta, the queen chanted silently for several moments until a soft blue glow appeared near her midsection, then flowed down her legs to the ground to the rhythm of her movements. Quickly the blue light coalesced atop the buried placenta, then the queen mother threw her arms out sideways, causing two shafts of blue to streak out, one towards each of the mounds. The light enveloping the placenta became a circle, then a straight line jutted out from the its bottom, forming a complete image of the ultimate symbol of life, the sacred Ankh.

As Keshef kept breathing and the Medjay women kept chanting and dancing, the blue Ankh rose slowly from the ground. Like a building, it stood upon a blue foundation nearly twice the height of a person, shimmering for all gathered to see. Then the queen mother lifted her chin, causing an ethereal replica of the placenta to emerged from the Ankh's circle. Queen Ah Hetep nodded towards the earth encased Nefertari and the ethereal placenta descended, disappearing inside the sacred mud. The queen's skin became slick with perspiration as she chanted and danced for several moments more. Then suddenly the Ankh silently exploded, showering the entire mountaintop in sparkling blue light.

As the light dissipated Keshef and Nefertari both screamed. The chants and dancing ceased and Queen Ah Hetep shouted:

"Get them out!" she cried, falling back into the arms of several women. "Get them out now!"

The Medjay women pounced upon both mounds and began tossing aside the earth. Within moments they pulled Nefertari loose, dashed her with water to clean off the mud, and found that her midsection was glowing a soft blue. It only lasted for a moment before it dissipated, then Nefertari surprised everyone by pushing her helpers aside to stand on her own two feet.

"Give me my baby!" Nefertari cried, throwing forth her arms.

Queen Ah Hetep took the child from the woman who held him and handed him to her. Nefertari cradled him gently as he looked up, cooing and gurgling at her with his large brown eyes.

"You shall be called Amen Hetep," Nefertari declared.

Then she looked toward the other mound

as they finally dug Keshef out. He was standing shakily, but as he leaned against the Medjay women he wore a broad relieved smile. Nefertari smiled back at him, looked around at all the women surrounding them, then said:

"Bless you my sisters! Thank you all for the healing of Het Heru! Now clean my man off and give him to me!"

The room was silent. Nefertari sat across the table from her Mut Queen Ah Hetep. Next to her sat Ahmesh. They had been left alone in this small room on the far side of the Medjay temple for nearly an hour, yet Nefertari still could not look up and into the eyes of her family. It had been days since the ritual that saved her life and that of little Amen Hetep and Nefertari had dodged this many times before her family finally cornered her. Keshef had pressured her also, so now she sat privately with her family after having told them of the past life revelation and the reason she had left Kemet. Nefertari had relayed it all, her tear filled eyes kept downcast in shame.

Long moments went by before her Mut broke the awkward silence.

"My child, look at me," the queen said. "Look at me now."

Nefertari shook her head as another tear slid down her cheek.

"I am not worthy to look at you..."

She cut an eye over at Ahmesh, to find him staring at her sadly.

"Nefertari you are my child and I still love you," Queen Ah Hetep replied. "Now look at me!"

Nefertari slowly lifted her head and looked into her Mut's eyes. Instead of the disgust she always imagined she would see, there was only sympathy. And love.

"I knew about your past life dear," the queen said.

Nefertari's eyes grew wide with shock.
"You did? But how?"

The queen leaned back, a smile coming to her lips

."My dear, I am a high priestess of Amen. I spoke to your spirit in the inner world between your incarnations. You agreed to come back through me and I was to train you to make amends for your past life. You should never have looked back at that before you were ready Nefertari. And you should have come to me after you found out about it."

Nefertari looked at her brother, doubtfully. He nodded, saying:

"Its true Nefertari. I was recruited through her womb also. We found the scroll after you left and Mut thought you had done the past life ritual and ran away. But we expected you to return soon after. Please come back home and we will work this out."

Nefertari shook her head sadly.

"What I did was...unforgivable. Mut, how could you consent to raise a monster such as me?"

"Every spirit is on a path Nefertari," the queen replied. "The creator's great work on earth takes many twists and turns and we all must play our part. Yours was to do evil in the past. Now your path is to make up for it. But I see that the pain of what you saw still has you in its grip. So I would like to address another issue."

"Which one!" Nefertari replied

.Queen Mut cocked an eyebrow.

"They will all be dealt with my child. Now I am speaking about the dark spirit that haunts you."

"My terrible sister..." replied Nefertari

."Yes," returned the queen. "She will be back and it may put Amen Hetep in danger."

"What must I do Mut?" Nefertari asked.

The queen thought for a moment.

"Your bond with this spirit is too strong for a common Ausar ritual. So we must take more permanent measures. A dark spirit cannot attack where there is an abundance of light. So we shall give you enough light to ward her off forever!"

"How are we to do this Mut?" Nefertari asked.

"We shall take Aten's very rays and infuse them inside of you," Queen Ah Hetep replied. "You shall undergo the ritual of the Eyes of Sekmet!"

High atop the sacred red mountain once again, Nefertari found herself at ritual anew in the renowned place of power of the Medjay people. This time instead of laying down covered with sacred earth, she stood upright, her head covered with a sparkling golden mask. She stood at the crack of dawn, as golden shafts of light blazed upon the fearsome visage she wore – a visage known to all Kushites that dwell near the great river Nile: lion headed Sekmet, protector of children, home and nation.

For the last 30 days at the very edge of dawn, then again at twilight, Nefertari looked through the eye slits of the mask directly into the waxing and waning light, absorbing the rays of Aten directly into her eyes. At first it was difficult, very difficult, due to the justified fear all living creatures had of gazing directly at the blazing orb or life. But the low light times of dawn and dusk, coupled with gazing through the specially designed mask did away with the harm, leaving only the accumulation of Ra force, the power of life. It was a rare and difficult undertaking, as Queen Mut Ah Hetep had explained the first morning Nefertari had been led through the ritual:

"There was a time, my daughter, when all the Children of Geb existed in a state similar to plants. We ate the rays of Aten with our eyes and did not consume things that grew or walked upon the land. But we lost that, and so much more, many, many ages ago. Some adepts maintained the secret knowledge of how to consume Ra this way even after the fall. They found that gold, particularly a golden mask such as the one you wear now, filters the raw power and helps Geb's Children to consume the nourishment from Aten directly once again. But we must take care! Our story about a raging Sekmet who steals the power of Ra is a tale of what happens when we tap this power with a troubled heart, making us vessels of power that could scorch the very land around us."

With that knowledge in mind Nefertari had stilled her heart with Men Ab meditation every night, then donned the mask at low light times to invoke the Eyes Of Sekmet. Just as her Mut had said, after the second week Nefertari's need for earthly food diminished and she found herself eating mostly to generate breast milk to feed little Amen Hetep. Two days into the third week, both Queen Muts stood beside her as she engaged the ritual, their eyes closed in con-centration as they laid hands upon Nefertari. Queen Mut Shem Sut opened her eyes first, followed by Queen Mut At Hetep. They nodded to each other, then stood with her as Aten went down and Nefertari took off the mask. As usual her head throbbed with swirling power, espe-cially right between her eyes. It was the Med-jay queen who spoke to her first:

"In all my days, including my own time in the ritual of Sekmet, I have never seen a being take to the Ra consumption the way you have my dear."

"What do you mean Mut?" asked Nefertari.

"She means that there are only a hand-ful of people known through out history who could consume Ra as efficiently as you do my daughter," said Queen Ah Hetep. "Our specula-tion is that your placenta ritual, combined with the power of this sacred place, along with some innate capacity gives you higher access to the power of Aten. But we shall contemplate this more later. It is time now to rid yourself of your dead Hyksos sister once and for all."

Just thinking about the spirit of her black eyed sister sent shivers down Nefertari's spine, especially since she now had Amen Hetep. The last time they had engaged in a battle of wills Nefertari had nearly succumbed and gone back over to the Hyksos. She wanted more than any-thing to be rid of this Dark Deceased, this Set empowered spirit from her past.

"How should I proceed Mut?" Nefertari asked.

"You must rest your head and go back to that place inside yourself," Queen Ah Hetep replied. "The place with the curtains that you described, where you were first approached by this dark spirit. With your eyes closed, you must lure her back into that little room. Then speak the puri-fication hekau and gaze upon her with the full force of the Eyes of Sekmet. She will not be able to withstand it. She will never return and per-haps you will even be able to enlighten her."

For several hours Nefertari did as instructed, imagining piece by piece, detail by detail the little room that she found herself in years ago when she had been near death during her ad-venture with Keshef and Ahmesh. Her Mut had told her that the place was likely had been a trap designed by her Dark Deceased sister to ensnare her for the Hyksos. Now it would be a trap set by Nefertari to be rid of her once and for all.

Nefertari felt herself being drawn down deep within, until she once again found herself stand-ing in the misty room with the ethereal, multi-colored curtains. After one quick glance to con-firm her location, she clamped her eyes shut and waited. Before long she heard a familiar voice calling out again from outside the curtains.

"Sister!" the voice cried. "You are back! Have you grown tired of being an outcast? Are you ready to come back to your people?"

Nefertari smiled slyly and answered:

"I don't know... I am tired of being alone and cast out."

"I knew you would come around eventually," her dead sister replied. "Do I have permission to come in?"

"Yes!" Nefertari replied.

Suddenly the dark spirit walked through the curtains. Nefertari could not see her because of her closed eyes, but felt her presence in all its palpitating evil. Nefertari sat calmly on the couch inside this spiritual room, her head bowed in feigned sadness. Her dead sister took a look at Nefertari, squinting her blacked out eyes.

"Wait! Why are your eyes closed sister? There is something different about you!" the dark spirit cried, stepping back. "You have given birth...and there is light in you..."

Suddenly Nefertari snapped her eyelids open, causing a tremendous blast of light to emerge from them. As the light crashed into her dark deceased sister Nefertari spoke the word of power:

"P-HAAT!"

Her dead sister screamed and tried to turn away, but Nefertari seized her, yanked her into a bear hug and held on tight. The spirit tried to break free, but Nefertari would not let go, as both their bodies shook like leaves in a strong wind. The entire room became a swirling vortex of power, as Nefertari's light struggled with her dead sister's darkness. Finally the light closed in, sweeping away the waves of dark, until only a small sliver of inky power surrounded the face of the dark deceased woman. Then even that dark mist drew into her blackened eyes. Nefertari then gazed into her fallen sister's black orbs, concentrating twin beams of light from her eyes into them. Her dead sister thrashed, screaming so loud it hurt Nefertari's ears, as the darkness in her eyes shrunk to pinpoints, before finally fading completely.

Suddenly the eyes staring back into Nefertari's were light brown, as they had been in their prior lifetime before the tragedy of the Set knowledge. Her sister smiled peacefully then, as her spirit dissolved into white smoke and began flowing away. Nefertari opened her arms to joyfully let her go, sensing that her twin from their prior incarnation had finally found peace. As the white mist that was her sister faded through the curtain a now soothing voice could be heard:

"Thank you my sister, you have saved me! I can now join our ancestors in a place of light! Receive now this gift I leave for you!"

Suddenly a barrage of images flowed through Nefertari's mind. After a few confused moments she realized that the images were of a place she had recently been taken to. She saw the history of the place, its organization, the placement of protective shrines and even its current troop strength. After sifting through the information, Nefertari woke up from her inner state to find both Queens looking down at her intently.

"It went well, I can tell my daughter," Queen Ah Hetep said. "I can sense you are no longer plagued by the minion of Set."

Nefertari looked up with a great smile.

"She is Set's minion no longer Mut. My sister is free and finally at peace. And as she departed she left me with a great gift also."

"What is it?" asked Queen Mut Shem Sut. "What was this great gift?"

"She has given me the means to destroy Set's Island!"

Chapter 11: I Spy Sea Maidens!

Nefertari knew exactly what to do with the revelations given to her by her deceased sister and immediately made plans to destroy Set's Keep. For the next moon she conducted military planning sessions in the early hours attended by Ahmesh, Keshef, Prince Pakhu, her Mut and other high ranking leaders among the Medjay and Kemits. All were astounded by her knowledge of details about the fabled Isle of Set. Not only did Nefertari possess a map that would lead them right to the hidden place, but she drew out attack plans that even a seasoned war general would envy from the information given by her dead sister. Nefertari was tireless, relentless and meticulous in the planning sessions which led all involved to hope that a serious blow could finally be struck against the tyranny of the Hyksos nation.

During one of these sessions a seasoned warrior named Apadi, a great Medjay general with broad shoulders and an imposing facial scar across his left temple, inquired about the Hittite girl who had come with Nefertari from the Set's Keep. All around the war table were surprised at Nefertari's uncommonly confused look.

"Hittite?" Nefertari replied. "How do you know she is Hittite? No one has been able to speak to her..."

Apadi gazed around the table with a puzzled look.

"I know what a Hittite looks like," he replied to the entire room. "They are one of the few unaligned countries. They are a mighty nation and I travel there every so often, trying to win them over to our side against the Hyksos. Now that I think on it, that girl resembles their queen, whose child was recently taken. Bring her in and I shall speak to her."

Nefertari sent Keshef to fetch Pudhukhpa. Upon arriving, she and Apadi immediately engaged in a lengthy conversation. Pudhukhpa seemed over joyed that someone could finally speak to her and looked to Nefertari with beaming smiles several times. Finally Apadi sat back and let out a long dramatic sigh.

"We have a princess on our hands," Apadi declared as everyone in the room gasped.

"I knew she must have been important somehow," Nefertari said, "but I did not dream..."

"She was taken during a diplomatic meeting with those dishonorable dogs, the Hyksos," Apadi went on. "When her people declined alliance they intended to punish them by killing her. She is a very brave little girl and fully intended to die until you freed her. She told me to thank you Nefertari."

Nefertari stood up from the meeting table, turned towards Pudhukhpa and threw open her arms. The girl ran over and they hugged for several moments. Their embrace was so filled with love that the eyes of everyone in the room watered. Nefertari let go of her, and then leaned over the table towards Apadi.

"Let us find out all she knows and then get her home," Nefertari declared. "Can you write in Hittite also Apadi?"

"Indeed I can,"he replied.

"Then we shall return her to her people with a proposal – an offer of just retribution against the Hyksos!"

As the days went by they continued to question the Hittite princess, who gave valuable information about her time on the evil island. Pudhukhpa warned especially about a black eyed woman of immense evil power, who took children away and never brought them back. All knew she spoke about one of the dreaded Set priestesses, who were powerful magicians that would have to be dealt with utilizing some strategy to be devised by the Queen Muts. After a week or so there was a tearful goodbye, then Apadi took Pudhukhpa back to her home.

During this time Nefertari also became devoted to her new life and family. Her nights were spent with Keshef and they were acknowledged as a married couple when Nefertari moved into his tent. This was the simple, respected mating protocol of the Medjay, though they discussed a more formal ceremony later in the style of Kemet. During the afternoons after the planning sessions Nefertari took Amen Hetep to be with his cousins. Though only 4 moons old and not yet crawling, he loved playing with the royal children and they adored giving their little cousin attention.

Each day Nefertari learned more and more about her new adopted people. And since she was a new Mut, her attention was especially focused on the lives of the young ones. One common form of play among the Medjay youth was the roping of the fierce mountain goats that lived in the nearby hills. Medjay children, especially the boys, loved to out do each other by catching the biggest and meanest goat in order to drag it to the corral inside the warrior's practice area. There they let the animals go, then took turns roping it again. There was a prohibited size rule handed down by Keshef and the other warrior teachers and most children adhered to it:

"If you can look it eye to eye leave it be!"

Each day, as the tough Medjay children scattered to the hills, Nefertari heard the seasoned warriors yell this after them, but, as with all youth, some did not listen. This happened nearly a moon later, on the day Apadi returned with the news that the Hittites would come in on the attack against Set's Keep. Plans to move out in a few days were drawn up and the

Medjay decided to celebrate by holding a goat roping contest among the young men. It was prince Pakhu's two boys, nine year old Heti and eleven year old Ba Teti who dragged an apparently oversized goat down from the rocks. The corral master closed the wooden gate behind them as Heti and Ba Teti dragged their prize past several goats brought in by the others. None of them had an animal that was half the size of the one the royal children dragged, which elicited envious looks from the other children.

Queen Mut Shem Sut, Queen Ah Hetep and Prince Pakhu sat next to Nefertari in chairs set apart for the royal family under the shade of a palm tree. Hundreds of others either stood or sat upon the ground watching. Keshef and Ahmesh were leaning on the wooden beams of the corral, looking on and shaking their heads.

"Do you want me to get the big one out of there?" shouted Keshef back at his brother.

Before he could open his mouth Queen Mut Shem Sut shouted:

"No don't you touch it!"

"But Mut," prince Pakhu cried. "The beast is clearly too large."

"They roped it and brought it down didn't they?" the queen replied. "Let them get their lumps for breaking the rules. Then the others will mind what we tell them..."

"But Mut, my sons could get hurt..." prince Pakhu replied.

"Good for them!" the queen shot back. "Goats usually go for the behind - correct?"

"Yes Mut." Prince Pakhu replied.

"Then let the beast soften up their rears as a consequence of their hard heads...just tell the corral master to be ready to keep them from serious harm."

Prince Pakhu opened his mouth to continue his protest, then thought better of it. He shook his head and waved his hand at Keshef, who nodded back. Then Prince Pakhu pointed at the corral master.

"I'll tell him to be ready," Keshef shouted.

As the first two Medjay boys released their goat, Keshef walked over to the corral master and pointed out the large animal brought in by his nephews. The corral master nodded and got up on his special platform with his own rope in hand. In the corral one of the boys acted as a decoy in the standard tactic, running up to antagonize their goat and taunting it by brandishing his butt. As usual the animal stamped its feet and ran up to the target, only to be stopped cold as the other boy tossed a rope over its head and yanked back. The taunter then tossed his rope over the creature's head and both boys yanked the goat to the ground. Each team was judged by the people for their skill, fearlessness and speed. There was no set prize, just an increased standing among peers and the respect of their teachers.

Nefertari sat holding Amen Hetep, enjoying the festivities. She laughed along with the rest of the crowd on the occasions that a rope missed, causing a young rump to be butted across the field. The children were taught to roll with the blow so no one was really harmed and the audience loved it. Watching a child being butted was the comedy all hoped to witness. But when Heti and Ba Teti untied their goat, a hush fell over the audience. The beast that stumbled to its feet was half a head taller that Heti, the tallest of the brothers. It was an angry male, with huge curved horns that looked like battering rams. The brothers showed no fear though and went on with the common tactic.

Ba Teti was younger and smaller, so he played the part of the target. The onlookers gasped as he ran around in front of the angry, stamping goat, which quickly charged. Heti spun his rope around in the air as his brother scampered away and threw. His timing was impeccable, his accuracy precise and Heti's rope floated over the creature's horns, landing about its neck. Heti dug in his heels and reared back, only to find himself ripped forward and dragged as the powerful beast yanked him effortlessly, then bore down to strike his little brother.

The beast struck Ba Teti hard in the rear, sending him sailing across the corral. It was a hard hit, but everyone expected the boy to roll and recover as usual. Instead little Ba Teti lay still in the sand. Struggling to his feet, Heti saw that the goat was poised to stomp down upon the still form of his little sibling. Wrapping the rope around himself, he jumped high into the air and came down, jerking the goat towards him. This only made the goat angrier and it turned its hate filled eyes on Heti. As it stamped it hooves, a second rope thrown by the corral master settle upon its neck. But the goat reared up high, then somehow stamped a cloven hoof directly on the new rope as it came down. This yanked the surprised corral master down from his wooden platform, causing the man to fall sideways and hit his head on a wooden beam on the way down. He lay prostrate in a daze as the goat kept charging.

By this time the crowd was on its feet, including Nefertari. As the goat chased Heti across the corral, Keshef and several other warriors jumped over the gate and charged forward, but it was clear no one would get there in time to stop the infuriated creature. Nefertari was breathless with concern. Because of her part in creating the child sacrificing Hyksos and as a new Mut, she was especially terrified about little Heti's plight. Suddenly something stirred inside Nefertari, a powerful throbbing in the pit of her womb that made her hand little Amen Hetep to Queen Ah Hetep. As she took the child, the queen looked at her daughter, noticing a faint blue glow near her midsection, as well as a yellow tint to her eyes. Just as the goat closed in on Heti, Nefertari leaped forward, throwing her arms powerfully to each side in the formation of the sacred Ankh. One of her hands touched the palm tree as Nefertari stamped her foot on the ground and screamed:

"Stop!"

Suddenly a line of green light leaped from Nefertari's midsection and flashed across the sand. Like a land based bolt of lightening, it streaked across the ground in an instant. The translucent green fire blazed right toward little Heti, forked around him, then reared up and spread out like a shield. The audience watched in amazement as the goat was violently stopped mid-stride, slamming into the green light as if it had hit a stone wall. Indeed, the animal crumpled up profoundly, breaking its horns, neck and both front legs. As the green light shimmered and faded away, the goat fell over, quite dead. Both queens looked on gaping, then looked back at Nefertari as the green light near her midsection and the yellow light in her eyes faded away.

The throbbing in Nefertari's womb subsided as she stood shaking her head, staring out at what she had done.

"I..I did not mean to," Nefertari said breathlessly. "I only wanted to stop it from hurting the child..."

Queen Mut Shem Sut and Queen Ah Hetep looked at each other in utter astonishment.

"This has not happened since the time of the ancients," muttered Shem Sut.

"And none ever expected that it would happen again..." Ah Hetep added.

"What!" cried Nefertari. "What is this? What has happened? Mut what have I become!"

"You have become a mighty power of creation Nefertari," her Mut replied, in awe. "The pure force of matriarchy personified..."

"Your Ra force from the Eyes of Sekmet

has blended with the Ankh force of the spiritual placenta my child," said Queen Mut Shem Sut. "You draw upon Aten and Geb together, blending them as one."

"But what is it," Nefertari asked desperately. "What does it all mean?"

Both queens leaned in, whispering in Nefertari's ears simultaneously:

"Wombfire!!"

Nefertari stood in the Medjay practice arena. Her knees were lightly bent in battle stance, her shoulders were loose and she spun her wombfire staff like a baton. The four Medjay warriors surrounding her were all very brave and had to be, because bones had been broken over the last several moons as she learned to control her gift.

One warrior grabbed a razor sharp dart from his belt and threw it at her, but the merest flinch of Nefertari's shoulder caused a wombfire shield to appear and stop it mid flight. She had learned to soften the green shields she projected and held the blade in midair instead of shattering it as she had done many times before. Nefertari then let it fall, while extending the wombfire back towards the thrower in the form of a battering ram. She imagined it as a large piece of wood, and so it seemed to onlookers that the warrior was hit by a translucent green log. He was blasted back off his feet and lay there in a daze.

The second warrior to press the practice attack came in with a famous Medjay power kick, leaping high and aiming for Nefertari's head. She lifted her chin and staff, then suddenly a green line corkscrewed up his leg from shin to thigh. The light held him in midair, then slammed him to the ground upon his back. Pinned down, he was left helpless and aching.

The third warrior had two sickle swords,

one on each of his hips. As he used both hands to reach across his body to draw them forth, no doubt to come at her with a double bladed attack, Nefertari waved her staff. Then both of his hands, along with his arms and legs, were suddenly pinned together as if he were in the grip of a great green fist. Indeed, a closed fist is what Nefertari imagined, so that is the form the wombfire chose to take. Nefertari lifted the man to eye level, spun him around and around, then set him down on the ground with his head spinning.

The last man stood before Nefertari to test her protective abilities in a combat situation. Concentrating on his body from head to toe, she surrounded him with a thin coating of green light just as an arrow shot from a concealed place struck his leg. But the warrior did not flinch, nor did he cry out. He shook his foot and the arrow simply fell away, having stuck itself not in his flesh, but in the sponge like manifestation of the green wombfire that surrounded it.

It had been difficult, because no instructions were left from the ancients on how to train a wombfire priestess. Indeed the people who carried the earliest oral traditions or wrote about wombfire in dusty tomes had never seen wombfire manifestations themselves. So the Queen Muts Ah Hetep and Shem Sut, who were also the highest of priestesses of each of their nations, did the best they could with the help of oracles and their own training. It was said that wombfire manifested in 4 ways: The protective placenta, the healing placenta, the striking placenta and the crushing placenta. Upon first glance it seemed wombfire came from the practitioner, but it was only guided by her. Taken from the life force of growing things, wombfire was directed by will and guided by the womb's natural mandate to defend, nurture and protect. Without any clear

Princess Nefertari

directions, there had been much trial and error in learning how to understand and control it.

At first Nefertari suffered from exhaustion and bad headaches after manifesting wombfire, until it was found that the closer to plants or water she was when extending her abilities, the less ill she felt. After checking with the oracles and much contemplation, it was discovered that water was not the key, but the plants that dwell within it. The details that had not been handed down was that wombfire comes through, not from the practitioner. Harnessed by Aten's rays derived from the Eyes of Sekemet, wombfire derived from the life force of plants. This was also a clue about how the knowledge of womb-fire may have been lost: the Kushite nations who recalled the tradition lived in areas that were formally wet, but now dry and largely devoid of plants. As the landscape dried up, creating wombfire priestesses would have become more difficult, until it may have been decided that the tradition was no longer meant to be.

The wombfire dependency on plants was a clue also about Nefertari's natural connection to the world of growing things revealed by her dead sister. To her Mut, it seemed reasonable to conclude that Nefertari's reincarnated closeness to the plant world was part of this spiritual path, and that the hardships she had endured were to hone her daughter to one day wield wombfire. So when she realized the nature of this gift and her daughter's attachment to it, Queen Ah Hetep took a traditional uas scepter and modified it, creating a perfect battle weapon for Nefertari.

Her wombfire staff, made from the strongest ebony wood, was hollowed out, its middle section periodically stuffed with fresh green plants and topped off with a solid gold head of Sekmet. The staff was then painted with a combination of sacred red earth from Nefertari's placenta ritual, special herbs and blood from Nefertari's moon menses. This gave Nefertari an even more precise spiritual blending with the wombfire, making directing it less taxing.

A cooling bin bin waist-let of white crystal encircled her midsection, ensuring that the more aggressive uses of her ability would not damage her womb. Finally, and most delightfully, Nefertari discovered that sacred sexuality techniques with a man of the bloodline that impregnated her was essential to help focus the wombfire. So as intimacies with Keshef empowered her, teachings from the Queen Muts informed her and the Medjay battle training prepared her, Nefertari was forged into a formidable weapon to counter the great power of the Hyksos witches.

And as for Nefertari, the training did more than develop new abilities. For the first time since her past life revelation, Nefertari felt strong, she felt like her life had meaning. And so, after nearly six moons of wombfire training, Nefertari, the Queen and the military council agreed: the time for the assault on Set's Keep had come.

Leaving Amen Hetep in the hands of his grand-Mut, Nefertari set out at the head of a war party that included two thousand Medjay warriors and nearly two thousand Kemetic warriors. This included 100 women, specially chosen by Nefertari from both Kemet and the Medjay, who were great swimmers and known for their skill with the bow. Utilizing carefully chosen pathways through the red hills, they marched to a secluded cove along the southeast corner of the Great Green sea. There they met Apadi with a fleet of ten warships from the Hittite nation. Upon boarding the lead ship, Apadi introduced Nefertari to a stern looking Hittite warrior. Nefertari could not understand him, but she saw how the seasoned warrior's face softened as he bowed deeply and gently took her hand.

"This is Mutallu, Nefertari," Apadi said during the introduction, "he is princess Pudhukhpa's older brother."

The man was very tall, and looked down at

Nefertari with a broad smile. He had the common olive skin tone of his people and long black hair tied in a tail. A great sword was strapped to his back and he had two daggers strapped to his left waist. Mutallu looked very formidable and under any other circumstance Nefertari would be concerned about close contact with him. But in this case she was glad to meet the brother of the little girl she had grown to love.

The Hittite prince spoke to Apadi for several moments, then let go of her hand and bowed once again.

"Mutallu is the leader of this fleet," Apadi said. "He is eager to avenge himself on those who stole his sister. He says that whatever you require shall be yours Nefertari."

Nefertari returned prince Mutallu's bow. Then the Hitite prince asked through Apadi:

"We have room for only two thousand of your men in this fleet. How are you going to get the rest to this island?"

Nefetari smiled and replied:

"Ask him if they have leather and leather workers in the fleet."

Apadi asked and Mutallu nodded affirmatively. Then Nefertari smiled with great satisfaction.

"Tell him we shall get ships from the enemy. But first I must call upon friends from the sea."

Following the map Nefertari took from Setja, they loaded a ship with elite warriors, including the carefully chosen bow women, then they sailed to an isolated island not far from the Set's Keep. After anchoring, Nefertari, Keshef, Mutullu and Apadi rowed to shore and set up camp on the beach. Immediately Nefertari chose a spot near the water and sat down cross legged. When questioned about what she was doing she simply instructed everyone to wait, knowing they would scarcely believe her explanation.

For days Nefertari spent her waking hours on the beach sitting in meditation. Even though the rising tide often rose to her chest she did not move. During the brief times she would open her eyes they glowed a strange yellow, similar to the rays of Aten. When they commented on this strange event Keshef informed everyone she was fine and directed them to simply leave her be.

Finally on the third day a dolphin with a white patch on its head appeared just off shore and Nefertari swam out to greet it. As Keshef and the rest of the party marveled, Nefertari and the dolphin somehow seemed to communicate. But this was nothing compared to the spectacle that developed over the next two days, as dolphin after dolphin came to join them.

When Aten rose on the fifth day, hundreds of dolphins surrounded Nefertari in the water just off shore. They jumped for joy and she swam all day with the creatures, before finally coming back near evening. Nefertari gathered every- one around her and they watched as she drew a curious design in the sand that was similar to a saddle for a horse. Then she look up and de- clared:

"My dolphin friends are with us in defeating those who hunt them. Have your leather crafts- men get to work on creating these riding devices and bring all the bow women from the ship to shore for training. We shall show the Hyksos something they have never seen before!"

The slave ship Apep was on its seventh run of the year to Set's Keep for another cargo of captives. Its captain, a gray bearded, bronze skinned Hyksos elder, stood upon the observa- tion deck enjoying the favorable winds and light- ness of the day. He felt good. He knew his ten percent take for the slaves would be lucrative, perhaps even enough to retire to that house in the mountains his belligerent wife had been nag- ging him about.

Straightening his red captain's sash emblazoned with the image of Set, he squared his shoulders and barked a useless order at a shipman simply because he felt like it. Just then he spotted something strange ahead in the water. He rubbed his eyes and squinted. What ever it was in the distance looked like a woman, yet also looked like a fish. Gazing up at the man assigned to the main mast for lookout, the captain shouted:

"Mast man! Just ahead to the left! What do you see?"

The lookout, who had been nodding off, scrambled to his feet in the lookout basket. He peered off in the direction the captain had indicated and gasped.

"Captain! I spy sea maidens!"

"What?" the captain shouted back. "Are you telling me you see women with fish tails mast man?"

"No captain! These are real women...riding fish!"

As the captain and rest of the crew ran over to the rails, the ocean all around the ship exploded with dolphin riding women. They were Kushite women, all quite naked, their brown and ebony skin glistening with sea water. The women smiled and flirted with the all male crew of the Apep as their dolphins rode the waves and dove back beneath the foamy waters time and again. The crew was loosing their minds with lust as they gaped at the beautiful women riding strange animals atop leather saddles. The straps wrapped around their shapely waistlines to secure them from falling off only added to their sensual allure. So when the women began to turn from away from the Apep's designated heading, the captain ordered the ship to follow. All aboard, including the captain himself, wanted to know the secret of the Kushite fish riding beauties.

Long entertaining moments went by as they were lured further off course. And the men leaned further over the ship's side, jostling with each other to get a better look. Then suddenly the naked beauties dove and were gone, immediately replaced by leather clad women with bows in their hands. Some of the men laughed, thinking the arrows being notched just more spectacle by imaginative harlots intent on luring them to an island of pleasures. Too late they came to understand, as wooden shafts shot from twanging bows embedded in their chests, that the teasing had stopped and an attack had begun.

The captain himself took an arrow to his arm, and shouted for his own archers to retaliate as he fell back onto the deck. As his bowmen ran forward and took positions to return fire, the dolphin riding attackers disappeared beneath the waves. The ship's bowmen peppered the water with arrows where they went under, but to no avail. Then suddenly, from another position very close the ship, a wave of dolphin riders blasted from the foam. Their dolphins leaping incredibly high, more leather clad women loosed a devastating barrage, decimating the ranks of the ship's bowmen. As they too disappeared beneath the waves loud shouting could be heard from the rear of the ship. The captain looked up from the bloody disaster of his devastated bowmen to find that, while they had been distracted by the shapely dolphin riders, a contingent of warriors had boarded.

The captain's heart sank more as he recognized the boarders consisted of a considerable contingent of the legendary Medjay warriors. He watched in dismay as the ebony death dealers cut through his crew like a knife through butter, peppering them with razor sharp darts, putting them down with expert swordsmanship and breaking bones with shattering kicks. There was also a woman with them, who wielded a staff with brutal efficiency and tossed men aside with what looked like some sort of green tinted magic. It was not long before those of his crew who where left alive surrendered, and he found himself face to face with the staff wielding Kushite woman. Stumbling to his feet, he clutched his arrow penetrated arm as the woman confronted him.

"You there!" the woman cried. "Were you the ships captain?"

The man straightened, pulled his sash around with his good arm and tried to stand with some sort of dignity.

"I am the ships captain!"

"No," the woman replied as she tore the sash from his chest. "You were the ship's captain."

Hours later the former captain found himself and the dozen or so men left from the Apep abandoned on a small island. Their captors were not cruel and made sure there was water, edible plants and a population of crabs to eat. The former captain hoped that someone at some point would discover them and was grateful, because he knew what he would have done with useless prisoners. So he assigned food gathering and hunting details, accepting that this island would be their home for the time being – or perhaps forever. He also accepted that, thanks to the staff wielding woman he somehow sensed was their leader, that he would surely not be getting his house in the mountains. But on the bright side, he mused, he may not ever have to hear his wife nag again.

Chapter 12: I am Set Priestess Nufa Nun!

The slave ship Apep, sailing under the maritime banner of Set, glided into the main port of Set's Keep. The vessel sat low in the water, indicating it was heavily laden with human cargo, causing the little man watching with scroll and stylus in hand to lick his lips in anticipation. A heavily laden ship usually meant a generous tip for the portmaster, especially one willing to ignore small improprieties and move registration along quickly. It just so happened that he was just such a portmaster.

As the anchor was tossed over and the gangplank extended, he checked the ship roster for the identity of the Apep's captain. Finding the name, the portmaster smiled, because this captain liked spending as little time in registration as possible, which meant a good bit of gold would be pressed to his palm this day.

But when those aboard the Apep started to disembark, the man wearing the captain's sash was not the person listed on the roster. Indeed, the tall olive skinned man was clearly not even a Hyksos, which was not unheard of, but highly irregular. The portmaster signaled to several guards and they walked with him over to confront the stranger, but they stopped upon viewing the human cargo being shoved from inside the ship. Dozens of ebony skinned men, clearly warriors in good health and of the highest caliber, were being brought down to shore. Upon closer inspection of the wrist bound, head bowed captives, the portmaster gasped.

"Medjay!" he cried. "You've managed to capture Medjay warriors? Who are you captain, and how did you come by this cargo?"

The man wearing the captain's sash stopped in front of the little portmaster, looking down upon him with impatience and disdain.

"Stand aside portmaster. My name is not

your concern," the captain declared haughtily. "All you need to know is that we were sent on a secret mission to acquire this cargo by the Great Three themselves."

The little man's eyes widened at the mention of the dreaded High priestesses of Set. He wondered if pressing this clearly powerful man would earn him a one way trip to their bloody alters. But he had a job to do and the penalty for not doing it was hanging for negligence. Besides, there had been no mention yet of his tip. Deciding patience to be the best route to payment, the portmaster waited as over one hundred of the finest human specimens he had ever seen were lined up for inspection.

Then the portmaster signaled to the waiting port surgeon, who had to call an assistant to help him examine all the new captives. The medical examination went on for long minutes as the captives were poked and prodded. Finally the surgeon nodded, indicating that the new slaves were disease free and healthy enough to be processed.

"No one told me about any mission, and a cargo of this richness is highly unusual." the portmaster said as he scanned the registration scroll. "You must at least give me some sort of credentials captain."

"I told you it was a secret mission good portmaster." the captain replied. "So you would not have known. We do have something that you will appreciate though...."

The captain signaled to several people standing just inside the cargo hold, then four strong men brought forth a huge chest. It was apparently very heavy, due to the strain they exhibited on the way down the gangplank. Finally they set it down at the feet of the portmaster and opened it up. The chest was loaded to the top with gold and silver rings, causing him to lick his lips vigorously, his eyes widening with glee.

"Take two handfuls portmaster," the captain said. "Then we offer you the honor of taking us into the main plaza, where we shall register this cargo in the name of the Three."

The portmaster's face truly lit up. This was the luckiest day of his life. Not only had this captain just made him rich, but he would become affiliated with the delivery of a rare cargo indeed. Medjay never allowed themselves to be captured alive, so any names associated with this great victory would be looked upon with much favor. After grabbing two handfuls of the rings and stuffing them into his waist satchel, he signaled for the warriors with him to assume honor guard formation around his generous new friends.

As the portmaster grandly led the Apep's contingent and captives away from the docks he informed an underling to hold all ship registration until he returned. He was so filled with greed and pride that he did not notice the unusual amount of ships arriving as he left. Had he noticed, it might have aroused his suspicion. Had his suspicion been aroused, the portmaster may have stopped an invasion.

Meanwhile, peeking out from the cracked door of the captain's cabin aboard the Apep, Nefertari watched the procession. Turning back around, she joined Keshef, Ahmesh, General Apadi and several others at a candle lit table. A map drawn by Nefertari of the entire island lay out before them, marked in several places. Nefertari's finger stabbed at some of the markings as she spoke in low tones:

"The rest of the fleet should be ready to move in from the east, north and west sides of the island to assist us. We all move when we get the signal from Mutullu and his infiltrators..."

"Do not worry about that Nefertari," Apadi said with a grim smile. "If my warriors know anything, its how to cause mayhem. They will attract all of the port's forces right to them and we will know when to make our go."

"I have all faith general," replied Nefertari. "First priority will be taking the Set Temple before they begin executing captives. I promised little Pudhukhpa I would free her friends and I will."

Keshef nodded.

"We are with you Nefertari and it will not be long," said the Medjay prince. "Indeed, all Medjay feel the anger that you do over the sacrifice of precious children. Mutullu and his men are just as angry about the kidnapping and threatening of his sister. Rest assured, the slavers in the plaza are about are about to feel Apademak's rage and Herukhuti's flame..."

"Captain" Mutullu and his men marched behind the portmaster and his guards into the plaza. As they went his disguised Hittite warriors and the seasoned Medjay pretending to be prisoners looked around, carefully assessing the battle strength of those guarding the place. Mutullu counted twenty five guards in the immediate area, only four of them bowmen. The portmaster marched them right up to a table next to a slave auction platform, where a squinty eyed administrator met them with a gaping mouth. The portmaster walked over and spoke to him, slyly pressing a silver ring into his palm. The administrator then waved back several other grumbling merchants and called Mutullu to the front of the line.

"I see you have a great many fine quality captives." the administrator said. "You wish to register them in the name of the Great Three?"

"No," Mutullu said. "I wish to make everyone here wealthy."

"Wealthy?" the administrator said asked in confusion. "How so?"

With great flourish, Mutullu beckoned the men hauling the heavy chest forward. Then he held his hands high and shouted so that the dozens of slavers and other merchants in the plaza could hear him.

"I said I have come to make everyone rich!" he cried. "I come to share it all!"

The men carrying the chest flung open the top, reached in, and started throwing gold and silver rings all around. Seeing the veritable shower of precious metal raining down, the merchants and many of the guards scrambled after them. After a few more handfuls were tossed, they began to wrestle with each other and fight. While the mad competition for free riches caught on like a fever, Mutullu and his men turned the chest over, spilling the weapons forth that had been hidden under the layer of rings.

Mutullu's men cut the hands of the Medjay captives free and tossed them the swords, throwing knife belts, arrows and bows. Mutullu drew his blade and the portmaster and administrator died first, their hands filled with the riches they so lived for. The rest of the guards dropped the rings and tried to pull weapons, only to be carved up by whirling blades. A few plaza guards on the far perimeter, who had failed to get in on the scramble, ran forward to attack, but were quickly cut down by Medjay bowmen.

Within moments the plaza was cleared of the guards, which only left the slavers themselves. Most were not warriors and stood with their hands up after the battle. Then suddenly their captives, who moments before were without hope of ever being free, seized the weapons of the downed guards and cut themselves loose. While Mutullu and the infiltrators ran from the plaza and dashed for the nearby administrative house, the slavers were being taken down by those who now saw a chance to take action. As horns blared from atop nearby rooftops to summon reinforcements, the captives set fire to several merchant stands. Those fires quickly spread and united, causing the plaza to became a blazing inferno.

The hundreds of Hyksos warriors guarding the port heard the commotion, then saw the flames in the plaza and ran towards them. This was the signal that the rest of the invaders were waiting for. The other invading ships saw the same thing, and those who were docked threw down their gangplanks, allowing hordes of Medjay, Kemetic and Hitite warriors to rush ashore. Dozens of other vessels, all acquired due to Nefertari's dolphin ploy, dispensed boats packed from stem to stern with ready fighters.

The invaders swarmed the docks like ants, cutting down any Hyksos who dared to stand in their way. General Apadi led the bulk of the forces to the north to prepare an ambush for the Hyksos regiments who would soon be arriving from the northern fort. Meanwhile Nefertari led Keshef, Ahmesh and a few carefully chosen warriors in a quick dash towards their destination: the temple of Set situated on the other side of the plaza. Nefertari was determined to get there before the witches who ran the place realized what was happening and started killing their stock of sacrifice victims, most of whom would surely be children.

As they skirted the blazing plaza, Nefertari and her warriors ran right into a contingent of ten or so Hyksos reinforcements. Both parties stopped, looked at each other, and then closed in to attack. Ahmesh and Keshef immediately jumped in front of Nefertari as two Hyksos warriors headed her way. One of them slashed high, causing Keshef to fling himself backwards, catching himself with one hand from falling on his back. He then snapped back up, delivering a kick to the man's throat. The warrior howled as his jugular was sliced by the razor sharp blade embedded in Keshef's sandal and as he went down Keshef's dagger followed him.

The Medjay prince turned from his dead foe to assist Ahmesh, to see two bronze skinned warriors dead at his friend's feet. The Kemetic prince was spinning his sickle sword, awaiting another large Hyksos who was running towards him with a huge cudgel. But a green wall suddenly appeared, which the hapless warrior smashed into full force. As the man crumbled to the ground Nefertari turned in several directions, flinging more wombfire all around. Slashing her staff parallel to the ground, she projected slabs of green force at the ankles of the enemy. Nefertari tripped them all, and as they went down a sharp Medjay blade or the butt of her ebony staff insured they stayed there. Due to this assistance from Nefertari, they made short work of the Hyksos contingent, then charged ahead toward the temple.

Looming ahead they saw a red painted building surrounded by a spiked wall. Like all things favored by Set, the temple was harsh, imposing and meant to be that way. Images of its long nosed, prominently eared patron surrounded by storm clouds were prominent, as well as monstrous renditions of snakes, hogs and hippos. They ran towards the building, only to see several red adorned men pop up atop the wall and begin shooting arrows. Nefertari and her warriors scattered, but one Medjay was badly wounded in the chest. As they dove behind thick bushes nearby, Nefertari knew she had to devise a hurried plan. Word had no doubt been relayed of the invasion, and the victims inside were at the mercy of the merciless.

After thinking for a few moments, Nefertari called out to Ahmesh and Keshef who were both hiding behind separate bushes. Ahmesh expressed doubts about what she suggested, but Keshef did not and her prince jumped out from behind his bush with confidence. He walked right up to the spiked wall as arrow after arrow rained down at him. A few actually connected, but the tips were absorbed by the green barrier that radiated from Keshef's body. As he got closer, Keshef took the bow from his shoulder, plucked an arrow from the shimmering protective placenta surrounding him and shot one of the red garbed warriors. There were three left up there, and they rained down arrow after arrow until Keshef resembled a green tinted pin cushion. But the Medjay prince just kept plucking the arrows, stringing them and shooting them right back. He shot one more red garbed archer in the neck, then the other two ducked down and disappeared.

Meanwhile Neftertari sat behind the bush, the butt of her staff stuck near the roots in front of her. She could feel the power of the plant seeping into her, filtering through her womb, and going out to Keshef like nourishment to an unborn child. As her brother ran forward to join him, she concentrated more and Ahmesh was covered with a green sheen of wombfire also. But protecting both was a great strain and she knew she could not keep it up for long.

Ahmesh ran up to the wall surrounding the building and tossed a grappling hook and line. As Keshef covered him by continuously firing arrows, he scrambled up the wall and jumped over. There were sounds of a struggle, then a red garbed man can flying over the wall, landing at Keshef's feet. A moment more and the thick door to the wall opened up and Ahmesh was standing there. Then Nefertari and the rest of their forces raced for the doorway, while a dozen or more red clad warriors came running from the temple. Walking behind them came two bronze skinned women clad in ebony garb. Both had inky black eyes.

`------------------

Warlord Komphis always enjoyed his mid-morning meal at the eating hall of the fort. So he was annoyed when they interrupted his dolphin steak and baby seal fritter platter with news of some sort of disturbance down at the plaza. He got slightly more angry after he heard of the slave uprising that killed all the slavers there. But he got downright incensed when he heard that there was a considerable force invading. So he finally pushed his meal aside and sent word for the rallying of the warriors of Sets Keep. He had 2500 battle hardened men ready to deal death to whomever had been foolish enough to invade this sacred abode. Then he'd get back to his meal.

Warlord Komphis commanded warriors who were incredibly well disciplined, so within the hour he was leading them in a brisk trot across the hilly landscape towards the docks in the south. He was not really worried, because he was sure the culprits were uncultured northern pirates who would scamper back to the sea at the sight of a superior force. These were men the Hyksos had come into contact with before, having hired them as muscle in the early days of the Hyksos empire. When they were no longer needed the barbarians had taken to plundering and there had even been whispers of them getting together in larger forces to attack richer targets. Good for them, Komphis mused, for the Hyksos themselves had started out the same way. Though he admired their pluck, he'd have to kill them for even thinking they could take Set's sacred island. The warlord was prepared to smite the pale skinned barbarians, and smite them hard, so when they marched around a hill and found the way blocked by hordes of black skinned warriors he was nearly struck speechless.

"Greetings Warlord Komphis," their leader said stepping forward. "I am general Apadi of the Medjay."

"But the Medjay are not a sea faring people," replied Komphis with smooth military coolness. "You are all desert dwellers."

"We have great sailors, have no doubt, but we do prefer sand dunes to sea waves," Apadi replied, with equal coolness. We were content to stay near those dunes until your people took to hunting us for spurning your alliance. I ask you now, leader to leader, to surrender."

"Why would I do that?" asked Komphis.

"Because there are 1000 warriors before you and if you look back, you will see 1000 more at your rear." Apadi replied. "And 3000 more coming over the surrounding hills..."

Warlord Komphis did look back. There he saw a considerable force behind them, blocking any retreat. He looked up at the hills and saw more pouring over.

"You have us surrounded," Komphis said. "Very clever and a classic move."

"Thank you for the compliment," replied Apadi politely. "Your answer?"

Knowing that he could never surrender, Warlord Komphis sighed. Then he and his men drew their swords. They would do their duty and fight to the end, as glorious sacrifices to Set. He just wished he'd finished that dolphin and baby seal platter...

Mutullu and the infiltrators secured the administrative building, posted guards near the door, then set off looking for the records of all the evil business done on Set's Keep. Nefertari had directed them to do so, because many considered this place to be mythical. If they could present the world with records of the Hyksos' monstrous wrong doings, in their own words, then the allies the invaders had acquired might be persuaded to abandon them. So as Medjay and Hyksos archers took up places on the roof and peppered arrows down on the arriving Hyksos reinforcements, Mutullu and a few others scoured the place for the records.

While running down a long hall towards the end of the building, a Hittite warrior called out that he heard something behind a closed door. Mutullu and several others joined the man at the door, finding it made of very thick wood reinforced with metal plates. They all heard battering sounds, indicating that someone was inside, possibly destroying needed evidence.

Mutullu called two axmen, who set about chopping through the door. As they chipped away, the sounds inside the room got louder and smoke started seeping out. It became apparent that someone inside was indeed destroying something, so Mutullu and the rest of his men began chopping at the wood with whatever blades they had along with the axmen. Suddenly the door started to shake, then the wood and metal began to ripple. As Mutullu was about to cry out to his men to get away, it blasted off its hinges, battering them to the floor and landing atop a few of them.

A piece of the metal from the door smashed him on the side of the head, causing Mutullu's vision to fade in and out as he fell back against a wall. Slowly loosing consciousness, he looked up to see a tall, copper skinned woman in all black striding from the burning room. She was completely calm, unafraid, and had what looked like a miniature storm cloud hovering over her. She walked over the bodies of his men, striding right atop the wooden door that had crushed them. One Medjay warrior struggled to his feet, but before his could pull one of his darts, a bolt of lighting hit him. The man burned to a blackened skeleton before he hit the floor. The final thing Mutullu saw before darkness overcame him was a pair of pitch black eyes looking down into his. Then he heard a terrible, terrible laugh.

Nefertari hung back as Keshef, her brother and the rest of the warriors engaged the temple guards. She noticed that the two black eyed women hung back also. Joining hands, they turned their faces skyward and a cloud started to appear above them. Nefertari recognized what they were doing from what had happened to the assassin band in the Kemetic throne room, and knew she had to do something fast.

She looked about quickly. Keshef, Ahmesh and their men had killed several of the Hyksos they engaged, while there was one dead Med-jay and a wounded Kemetic warrior. An atef was dragging their bodies to protection behind a tree. A tree! Nefertari sprinted over to it, just as the black eyed women called their men back, and stuck the butt of her staff down into the cluster of roots at her feet. As soon as their warriors were safely behind them, the black eyed women threw up their hands and the cloud over them rumbled and sparked.

"Get down!" Nefertari cried.

Keshef, Ahmesh and their men threw them-selves to the ground, covering their heads as best they could. Concentrating with all her might, Nefertari projected a great green image of a placenta above them just as blasts of light-ning poured down into it. The protective placenta rocked back and forth, and Nefertari felt pres-sure in her own womb. Drawing more upon the tree's power, she continued absorbing the light-ing, while slowly turning the green oval shield, pushing it closer and closer to the storm cloud.

The women looked up at the green placenta and renewed their efforts. This time they shout-ed words of power, shaking their fists in anger. Nefertari pushed harder, causing the placenta of power to completely envelope the cloud and it's lightning. Mouths gaping, the women looked up at their captured magic, looked over at Nefertari in wide eyed disbelief, then conjured until the storm blazed more intensely. Blast after lightening blast assaulted the green barrier, and it continued to hold, but Nefertari felt a pressure akin to a watermelon in her womb and knew she had to end the conflict quickly.

Suddenly she got an idea and grasped her staff tighter. Shaking with perspiration, Nefertari positioned the ethereal placenta directly over their enemies heads. Then, flexing the same womb muscles she used to give birth, she opened up the bottom of it. Thrusting her pelvis she pushed, and the great placenta dropped like a cup on top of the Hyksos witches and their men.

Nefertari then focused on the tension she felt building in her womb. Breathing deeply, she shoved the pressure away, causing the pent up lightning in the spiritual placenta to discharge violently. Shrieking and howling as bolt after bolt was release into them, the Hyksos jerked back and forth until they fell and shrieked no more. A few moments went by as Nefertari waited for the storm to subside, then she dissipated the womb-fire power and leaned back against the tree in exhaustion.

Ahmesh, Keshef and their men walked over and looked down. Where the Hyksos witches and their men once stood there were only ashes. Then they looked back at Nefertari, amazed at the extent of her powers. Ignoring their stares, Nefertari pushed to her feet and took off for the building. Then the rest of them quickly followed.

Storming into the temple, they first looked around for more resistance. Finding none, they ran past the outer room, down a long hall and towards the main alter room. All along the way there were foul images on the walls of Hyksos witches sacrificing people, mostly children, and they feared what they would see ahead. Finally bursting into a huge hall, they saw a large alter on a raised platform. A big red handled knife was sitting atop it, no doubt ready for the grim tasks of taking innocent life in the name of Set.

A little fat man in red and black came waddling out from behind the alter. He was wide eyed with fear and shouted with indignation.

"Get out!" he cried. "You can't be here!"

"Where are the children little man," Ahmesh said, stepping forward menacingly.

"You can't have them!" the copper skinned, round face man cried. "They belong to her. She will kill me, or worse if I let you take them!"

Keshef stepped forward, took out a dart and threw it. The blade impaled between the little man's toes.

"Owww!" he cried, clutching his foot. "Why did you do that?"

"The next one goes between your legs," replied Keshef calmly. "Show us where the captives are."

"I'll never tell!" the little man howled as he rolled around in pain. "Never!"

Nefertari started to say something, then she felt a twinge in her womb. The image of little Amen Hetep flashed through her mind, and she had the feeling she had when her child was hungry or needed to be changed. Then a small strand of green emerged from her staff and moved along the floor like a snake. It twitched for a second, then began heading towards a wall hanging on the far side of the room.

"No!!!" cried the little man as he watched the movements of the strand. "She forbids it!"

Nefertari, intensely concentrating, waved her hand at the little whining man.

"Silence him." she said.

Ahmesh walked up to the little man and hit him once in the face. He gasped and crumbled to the floor.

The green strand wound right up to the wall hanging, then went under it. Keshef yanked the hanging down, revealing a large door. He then signaled two large, strong Medjay and they ran up to the door and kicked it down. They entered to find a large, torch lit room full of cages, dozens of them, and inside the cages were children.

They all were naked, sitting or laying atop filthy piles of hay. Water bowls were the only other thing inside with them. Nefertari's eyes teared up at the sight of such cruel, animal like treatment. As they walked into the room all the children cowered to the back of their cages. Most looked like they had not bathed in weeks or longer. Their eyes were terrified and hopeless. Nefertari walked up to a cage that held a little ebony skinned boy. He looked to be around seven, and began crying as she came near.

"Its alright little atef," Nefertari said soothingly. "We won't hurt you."

The little boy curled up into a ball near the back of the cage, continuing to weep and snivel. Nefertari walked back to the men, who wisely waited near the door.

"Who has rations?" she asked.

Ahmesh opened a small satchel on his hip and pulled out several bits of dried fruit. He handed it to Nefertari and she walked back over to the little boy's cage.

"Look atef, I have some food." she said bending down with it.

The little boy looked up. Then all the other children in the cages leaned forward, looking on hungrily. Nefertari handed the food to the little boy and he mashed it into his mouth. Then all the children started reaching through the bars, hungrily begging for food. Nefertari smiled and they began smashing through the wooden cages. Once freed, the children were enticed from the room with the promise of more food. As they made their way back through the sacrifice hall, they noticed a body atop the alter. It was the little man who tried to stop them. His hands were wrapped around the handle of the large sacrificial knife, its blade plunged deep into his chest. As they left Nefertari shook her head, wondering what could inspire such desperate fear.

Moments later they were marching through the entrance of the temple with nearly one hundred children in tow. All were between two and eight years old and mostly from Kemet. Most had been kidnapped, some had been sold and others had been bred from servants of the Hyksos in Avaris. The poor children had been given nothing but bread crusts and water in captivity, some for over a six moons. All were to be slaughtered like sheep by a black eyed lady they all feared terribly.

They met Apadi when they marched past the smoking ruins of the plaza, who informed her that the army of Set's Island had been de-stroyed. The island was subdued, he reported, but prince Mutullu was missing. Then Apadi's men gave all their rations to the hungry little children.

As they neared the port, they noticed their forces plundering the ill gotten gains of the island, which was just as it should be. The plan was to take the riches of the place, ban-ish those they found and burn Set's Keep to the ground. They observed hundreds of Hyksos merchants and slavers begging to have their possessions returned. But it was not to be. All riches were to be distributed equally between the Medjay, the Hittites, the Kemits and used to compensate those freed from bondage.

As they neared the docks a discussion be-gan about sending searchers to find price Mu-tullu, when suddenly they heard his voice.

"Flee Nefertari!" Mutullu screamed in a pained and anguished voice. "Run while you can!"

Looking around for Mutullu, Nefertari and the rest saw a strange and terrible sight. Right near the port entry there was a huge pile of bodies. The dead were ebony skinned Medjay, olive skinned Hittites and brown skinned Kemit warriors. And atop the bodies stood a tall copper skinned woman with black eyes and a terrible face. A face that radiated untold evil. She held Mutullu by the throat with one hand as if the big man weighed nothing. Then she tossed him aside like a ragdoll and he rolled down the pile of bodies.

"So it is you!" cried the Hyksos witch. "This fool was telling the truth! You are behind this desecration!"

Everyone with Nefertari drew weapons and a hundred arrows were suddenly pointed at the fearsome woman. But she simply laughed and waved her hand, uttering a harsh sounding word of power.

Suddenly fear such as none of them ever knew before gripped all within sight of the witch. Hands shook, knees knocked and strong warriors whimpered like children. Everyone dropped their weapons as the Hyksos witch walked down the pile of bodies like a set of stairs.

"You feel the fear," the harsh, hate filled voice of the witch cried. "The justified fear of those who oppose Set. I have unleashed the collective terror of a thousand sacrifices upon you. The delicious moment just as the blade falls, when they know that Set shall devour them. None can withstand it. Now kneel."

Nearly a thousand warriors started getting down on their knees. All except Nefertari, who, though she felt just as much terror as the rest, called upon the power of wombfire to fight against the witch's mental enslavement. Even Keshef and Ahmesh bowed down, though the beads of sweat pouring from their brows indicated they were fighting with all their might.

"Ha ha," the witch laughed, pointing at

Nefertari. "You resist. It is no less than I would have expected from the progenitor of all the Hyksos. I salute you, great ancestor, before I kill you."

"You...you know me?" Nefertari replied. "But how?"

"It was I who sent the blundering fool Ten Na to fetch you when you were a young girl," the witch replied with a terrible smile. "And when that failed I pulled your dead sister from the inner realms in hopes that she could convince you to come back to us. The Hittite assassins who almost succeeded in getting you were sent by me also. I am Set Priestess Nufa Nun of the Dread Three!"

"What???" Nefertari cried angrily. "It was you! You are responsible for all this torture in my life!"

"Not torture, Nefertari, but seasoning," the witch replied. "A grooming process for you to return to your people. We of the Dread Three hoped you would return and lead us to more glory in this lifetime. But your stubbornness and the power of your retched Mut destroyed those plans."

"No!" Nefertari cried, raising her staff. "I shall destroy you witch!"

With a twitch of the witch's hand, a strong whirling wind wretched the staff from Nefertari's grasp and sent it flying through the air. Then a lightning bolt from a newly formed storm cloud struck it and the staff shattered into small pieces. Suddenly the witch raised her arms and the cloud began to grow.

"I shall destroy all those you hold dear Nefertari," Nufa Nun cried. "Your brother, your husband and all those who were foolish enough to follow you to this sacred place. Then, when you are on your knees weeping, you shall join them."

Nefertari looked up at the witch. Then she looked back at her husband, brother and all